P9-CKR-172

Definitely!

PROBABLY

Maybe Unicorns here

THE UNICORN RESCUE SOCIETY

THE SECRET OF THE HIMALAYAS

THE UNICORN RESCUE SOCIETY

THE SECRET OF THE HIMALAYAS

BY **Adam Gidwitz & Hena Khan**

ILLUSTRATED BY **Hatem Aly**

CREATED BY **Jesse Casey, Adam Gidwitz, and Chris Lenox Smith**

DUTTON CHILDREN'S BOOKS

DUTTON CHILDREN'S BOOKS

An imprint of Penguin Random House LLC, New York

First published in the United States of America by Dutton Children's Books,
an imprint of Penguin Random House LLC, 2021

Library of Congress Cataloging-in-Publication Data is available.

Book manufactured in Canada
ISBN 9780735231450

1   3   5   7   9   10   8   6   4   2

Edited by Julie Strauss-Gabel
Design by Anna Booth
Text set in ITC Legacy Serif Std

To the Unicorn Rescue Society:
Joe, David, Emma, Hena, and, especially,
Hatem, Anna, Julie, Chris, and Jesse.
—A.G.

To Azim. You are the GOAT.
—H.K.

To family & friends currently too far to reach,
with love.
—H.A.

UNICORNS ARE REAL.

At least, I think they are.

Dragons are definitely real. I have seen them. Chupacabras exist, too. Also Sasquatch. And mermaids—though they are *not* what you think.

But back to unicorns. When I, Professor Mito Fauna, was a young man, I lived in the foothills of Peru. One day, there were rumors in my town of a unicorn in danger, far up in the mountains. At that instant I founded the Unicorn Rescue Society—I was the only member—and set off to save the unicorn. When I finally located it, though, I saw that it was *not* a unicorn, but rather a qarqacha, the legendary two-headed llama of the Andes. I was very slightly disappointed. I rescued it anyway. Of course.

Now, many years later, there are members of the Unicorn Rescue Society all around the world. We are sworn to protect all the creatures of myth and legend. Including unicorns! If we ever find them! Which I'm sure we will!

But our enemies are powerful and ruthless, and we are in desperate need of help. Help from someone brave and kind and curious, and brave. (Yes, I said "brave" twice. It's important.)

Will you help us? Will you risk your very *life* to protect the world's mythical creatures?

Will you join the Unicorn Rescue Society?

I hope so. The creatures need you.

Defende Fabulosa! Protege Mythica!

Mito Fauna, DVM, PhD, EdD, etc.

CHAPTER ONE

It was an exciting day in Miss Vole's class. Pai Lu had published the school's first-ever student newspaper, and she was sharing the debut issue:

"I call it the *End Times*!" she announced dramatically. She raised the paper into the air.

"Oh!" said Miss Vole. "Like the *New York Times* or the *Los Angeles Times*!"

"Right," Pai Lu agreed. "Except it's the *End Times* because the world is about to end."

"Oh, Pai Lu!" Miss Vole scoffed. "That's not

true! Earth will last for billions and billions of years!"

"Unless the *zombies* get us."

"What?!"

"Or the moon drifts off course and smashes into the earth."

"That's not going to happen!"

"Or werewolves," Pai Lu said, tapping her chin. "Maybe the werewolves will come before the zombies."

Uchenna, a cheerful punk-rock girl with

dark twists in her hair, leaned over to her best friend, Elliot. "Pai Lu has kind of a dark outlook on life."

Elliot, a curly-headed boy who wore identical polo shirts and khaki pants to school every day, nodded as he scribbled notes.

"What are those?" Uchenna asked.

"Now that I'm editor of the Proceedings of the Unicorn Rescue Society," he whispered, *"I need to learn more about periodical publishing."*

Elliot and Uchenna were members of a

secret society whose mission was to save mythical creatures—like dragons, Sasquatch, and sea serpents—from danger. The society's headquarters were in the basement of Elliot and Uchenna's school, and its founder was their social studies teacher, Professor Fauna. He was a pretty weird dude.

"So," said Pai Lu, "you put the most important articles on the front page. Like, 'When will the zombies get us?' And 'Will a piano fall out of the sky and crush you? Maybe, says local statistician.'"

A girl named Shruti said, "I'm getting freaked out."

"I think we all are," agreed Miss Vole.

Pai Lu went on: "I call that the *Bad News* section. There's also *Lifestyles and Deathstyles* . . ."

A small shriek escaped Miss Vole's lips.

". . . *Pointless Physical Exertion*, aka 'sports' . . ."

"Hey!" cried Johnna, star of the soccer team. "And *About Town*."

Uchenna and Elliot looked surprised. That one seemed uncharacteristically normal.

"I need a better name for that section," Pai Lu admitted.

Miss Vole, very nervously, said, "Do I dare ask what articles you included in your premier issue? Actually, maybe I don't want to kn—"

"Well," said Pai Lu, "in addition to 'When will the zombies get us?' and the random falling piano article, we have a recap of last week's soccer game, which our team had to forfeit because Jimmy kept picking up the ball and running off the field."

"The out-of-bounds lines are *not clear*!" Jimmy protested.

"Yeah, but why'd you keep picking up the ball with your *hands*?" Johnna complained.

"And then running into the parking lot and punting it across the street?" added their friend Jasper.

Jimmy grinned and shrugged. Johnna folded her arms and glowered at him.

Uchenna leaned over to Elliot again. "It was definitely the most *entertaining* soccer game of the year."

"What else is in your newspaper, Pai Lu?" Miss Vole asked, valiantly maintaining her daily, desperate, futile struggle to keep her students on task.

"Eh. The rest isn't that interesting. I did an interview with these local guys called the Schmoke brothers. I try to print articles that challenge the readers' assumptions. And mine! But this was one article where my assumptions were completely right. They looked like boring, money-obsessed business dudes, and they—"

BANG!

The door slammed open. Shruti squealed, "Zombies!" Miss Vole shouted, "Werewolves!" Jasper cried, "The moon!"

"EXCUSE ME, MISS VOLE!"

Standing in the doorway was a tall man with wild hair, a salt-and-pepper beard, and a frantic look in his eyes.

It was Professor Fauna, the founder of the Unicorn Rescue Society.

CHAPTER TWO

"YOU!" Professor Fauna said, pointing at Pai Lu. "Did you write this newspaper?!" He was holding a copy of the *End Times* in his fist.

"Uh . . . yes?" said Pai Lu.

Professor Fauna stormed up to the black-clad newspaper editor and came so close that his beard hairs touched her eyebrows. "And do you *swear* on your young life that everything you say in here is true?"

"Um . . . I mean, the statistics on the falling pianos are just probabilities, so I can't claim . . ."

"Not that! Though that was a sobering article to be sure. It really made me think. . . . But no! I am talking about the interview with the Schmoke brothers!"

"Oh," said Pai Lu. She straightened her back and glared up into the professor's eyes. "I have journalistic integrity. Everything in there has been fact-checked and confirmed. Responsible journalism is how I keep the darkness at bay. Also the werewolves."

Professor Fauna turned around and scanned the room until his gaze came to rest on Elliot and Uchenna. Then, in a whisper so loud people in the school cafeteria could probably hear it, Professor Fauna said, *"She has written an article about the Schmoke brothers! She has been in their house! Spoken to them! And published crucial information about my enemies . . ."*

He suddenly stopped. Everyone was staring at him, openmouthed.

"The Schmoke brothers are your enemies?" Pai Lu said. She whipped a notepad and a pen out of her back pocket. The notepad was decorated with skulls. "Maybe my assumptions were wrong, and there *was* something interesting there. . . ."

"Enemies?" Professor Fauna said, with a fake innocence that fooled exactly nobody. "Who said 'enemies'?! I did not! Not me!"

He looked desperately at Uchenna and Elliot. They held up their hands in a gesture that said, very clearly, *You're on your own.*

Professor Fauna forced a laugh. "You thought I said 'my enemies'! Hahaha! Of course not. I was saying . . . *anemones*! Yes! I am in a rock band with the Schmoke brothers, and we call ourselves the Anemones!"

"You and the Schmoke brothers? That sounds like the worst rock band ever," said Johnna.

Jimmy asked, "What instrument do you play, Professor?"

Professor Fauna looked like he suddenly couldn't think of a single musical instrument. "Um . . . the bassoon! Anywhat, I need Elliot and Uchenna to come with me right away."

Miss Vole objected. "Professor Fauna, you are *always* taking those two out of class! It is *highly* inappropriate!"

"I *could* sing you a song by the Anemones...," he said. "We do a very good cover of 'It's Raining Men'!"

Jimmy piped up. "I'd like to hear that."

Miss Vole let her head fall to her chest. She sighed. *"Just go."*

As they hurried down the hall, Uchenna heard Jimmy start to sing, *"Tonight for the first time ... just about half past ten ... for the first time in history ... it's gonna start raining men ..."*

CHAPTER THREE

U chenna and Elliot followed the professor down the steps to the basement, and then down some more steps to the subbasement, where the international headquarters of the Unicorn Rescue Society were located. In a janitor's closet, which Professor Fauna had claimed as his office.

At least, they tried to follow him. But he was *sprinting*. He even ran past the school principal, Ms. Kowalski, who shouted, "No running in the halls!" as Professor Fauna pelted past. Uchenna and Elliot hurried after him as fast as they could without actually running themselves, which made them look kind of like penguins. Principal Kowalski glowered at them as they waddled by.

Down in the subbasement, they were able to run again, and they caught up with Professor Fauna just as he threw open the door to his office. Two walls were covered with bookshelves. The third wall had old charts and even older letters and sparkly pink sticky notes all over it. Multicolored yarn zigzagged from document to chart to note to chart again. It looked like Professor Fauna was trying to crack one of the world's greatest mysteries.

Which he was.

"Hey," said Uchenna. "What's wrong with Jersey?"

A small, furry blue creature with red wings, a face like a goat's, claws on his forelegs, and hooves on his hind legs was cowering under the desk.

"He's trembling!" Elliot exclaimed, scooping

up the little Jersey Devil. "What happened to him?"

"What happened to *him*?" Professor Fauna shouted. Which made poor Jersey tremble and try to crawl inside of Elliot's sweater. "I screamed, is what happened to him. And continue screaming. But the important question is: What happened to *me*?! And my life's work?! Read this!" Professor Fauna thrust his copy of the *End Times* into Uchenna's hands. "Just read it and tell me that the world is not ending!"

"Not the falling pianos again," Uchenna murmured.

"Not that! This one!" He jabbed at an article with his finger.

MAKES YOU WANT TO "RECHE":
AT HOME WITH THE SCHMOKES

by Pai Lu

Last week, I sat down with the billionaire Schmoke brothers, Edmund and Milton, in their home, to learn more about two of the richest citizens in our town.

We sat in their elaborate "parlor," which was different from their "living room," their "sitting room," their "receiving room," and their "den."

I assume the parlor had walls and a floor, but they were impossible to see through the thick rugs, gold-encrusted light fixtures, and oil paintings of the Schmoke brothers doing things like riding horses and posing with gold bars.

Milton Schmoke and Edmund Schmoke told me all about their various businesses. Logging, construction, pharmaceuticals, money laundering, hospitality . . .

I asked them about a strange horn that stood on the mantel above their fireplace.

Talking about the horn made the Schmoke brothers excited, like dogs about to be fed from a can. They told me they got it in the Pakistani Himalayas, through their new business venture, which involves taking unbelievably rich people on hunting expeditions for unbelievably rare creatures.

As Edmund Schmoke

explained: "Our slogan is 'See animals like you've never seen them before! And never will again!' We call the company Rare and Exotic Creature Hunting Expeditions, or RECHE, for short." He pronounced it "reach."

"Like 'reach for your dreams!'" added Milton Schmoke.

I asked: "Wouldn't *R-E-C-H-E* be pronounced 'retch,' like what your 'rich people hunting rare animals for fun' business makes me want to do?"

I then proposed Rich People Hunting Rare Animals for Fun as an alternative name for their company, with the nifty acronym RPHRAFF for short. Pronounced "riffraff."

The Schmokes invited me to leave. It was the best thing that happened all day.

"There!" Professor Fauna cried. "Do you see?"

"See what?" said Elliot.

"That Pai Lu is way funnier than I thought she was?" Uchenna said. "We should totally start hanging out with her."

"*Don't you see what this MEANS?!*" Professor Fauna was still screaming. Jersey shoved his head into Elliot's armpit for safety. "*Look at the photograph!*" the professor cried.

Elliot and Uchenna brought the photocopied newspaper close to their faces.

There was a photo, taken by Pai Lu, of the Schmoke brothers. They were grinning proudly, standing in front of their fireplace. And up on the mantel, just behind Edmund's left shoulder, was a horn.

A very distinctive horn.

"That looks like . . . ," Uchenna murmured.

"A whole *lot* like . . . ," Elliot went on.

"A unicorn horn," they both said at once.

"*OF COURSE IT DOES!*" Fauna wailed. "And

that means they have KILLED one! Those evil, greedy, selfish, immoral, amoral, *jerk-faced* brothers *traicioneros, mezquinos y malévolos* have found a unicorn! Before I did! And they have KILLED IT. *I WILL NEVER FORGIVE MYSELF!*"

Professor Fauna collapsed on the floor in a ball, weeping and tearing at his hair.

"Professor!" Elliot and Uchenna knelt down beside him. "Professor!"

Uchenna said, "You don't *know* that it's a unicorn horn!"

"Yeah," Elliot agreed. "It could be from a narwhal."

"In the Himalayas?" Professor Fauna exclaimed.

"Okay, not a narwhal. Maybe a goat?"

"With a single horn? A single, beautiful, straight, spiraling horn? And you think that the Schmokes are taking their rich friends to hunt rare and exotic *goats*?"

Elliot had to acknowledge that this was unlikely.

Professor Fauna jumped up and grabbed Uchenna and Elliot by their shirts. Jersey flapped away frantically to hide on top of a bookshelf. He covered his eyes with a red wing.

"Do you remember the old blind man from the Archives in Havana?"* Professor Fauna asked. "Juanito?"

"Of course," said Uchenna. "You don't meet a blind librarian every day."

"Especially one who has the contents of the library's books and papers completely memorized," added Elliot.

"*Exactamente!* And Juanito told me what he

---

* See *The Madre de Aguas of Cuba.*

remembered from the papers of the Secret Order of the Unicorn! Namely, that the unicorns have long, straight, spiraling horns. Like this one!" He stabbed the photograph with a finger.

"And that a mature unicorn's horn is approximately three feet long! Like this one!" He slapped the paper.

"And that they live in the highest mountains! Like—"

"The Himalayas," Uchenna and Elliot said in unison.

"*Claro*. So this *is* a unicorn horn. The Schmoke brothers *have* found them, and are *hunting* them, and my life has been a *waste of time*!"

Professor Fauna started sobbing again.

Elliot and Uchenna looked at each other. And they smirked.

"WHAT?" Professor Fauna demanded, seeing them. "What on earth is there to smile about?"

Uchenna said, "We *are* members of the Unicorn Rescue Society, are we not?"

"Yes! So?"

Elliot said, "And we have never even seen a unicorn. Right?"

"*Why do you insist on rubbing it in?*" the professor wailed.

"Um," said Uchenna, "don't you think it's time we, I dunno, *rescued some unicorns?*"

Professor Fauna sat up. He looked back and forth between the two children.

He sniffed. Then he wiped his tweed suit sleeve savagely across his nose.

"You are right," Professor Fauna said. "You are right! How can I have been so foolish? This is the chance of a lifetime! We will see the unicorns at last! And save them from my enemies!"

"Your rock band?" Uchenna asked.

Ignoring her, Professor Fauna leaped to his feet. "Let us do it!"

"Yes!" cried Uchenna and Elliot.

"We shall go," Professor Fauna bellowed, "and save the unicorns!"

Jersey swooped down from the top of the bookshelf and landed on Professor Fauna's outstretched arm. He let out a tiny crow of enthusiasm.

"Okay!" said Elliot. "So we're going to the Himalayas. To save some unicorns. We can do this. Let's plan today, talk to our parents tonight, make sure our passports are up to date, look for flights on safe, commercial airlines . . ."

"Ha ha ha! My silly young friend!" The professor laughed. "We have no time to lose! The unicorns need us! To the *Phoenix*!"

Uchenna and the professor rushed out the door, Jersey flapping ahead of them, toward the school parking lot and their tiny, single-propeller airplane.

Elliot sighed. "It was worth a try."

CHAPTER FOUR

For a brief moment, just minutes ago, Elliot had experienced a feeling that could only be described as glee. They had probably discovered the location of a herd of unicorns, and they'd decided to save them. They would finally fulfill their mission as members of the Unicorn Rescue Society!

But now Elliot was strapped into Professor Fauna's rickety airplane. The *Phoenix* was hardly bigger than the canoe sitting in his next-door neighbors' driveway. And any earlier glee was replaced with all kinds of *other* feelings.

Like, that he was quite certain the plane was going to crash somewhere between New Jersey and Pakistan, and that they would all perish horribly and painfully.

"This is *awesome!*" Uchenna said, pumping her fist. "Unicorns, here we come!"

"I agree!" Professor Fauna shouted over the roar of the propeller. "Unicorns at last!"

Elliot's pulse was racing faster than the plane was barreling through the teachers' parking lot.

"Is there a blood pressure monitor in the first aid kit?" Elliot yelled, wiping beads of sweat off his forehead. "My heart is beating too fast! I think it might explode!"

"First aid kit?" Professor Fauna roared over the rattling of the plane as they picked up speed. The plane sputtered and lurched into the air, right before they would have slammed into the side of the school gym. "What first aid kit?"

Elliot rifled through his backpack for a bag to breathe into, but the only one he found was filled with pretzels. Which Jersey, of course, wanted immediately.

"Are we really going to fly to the *Pakistani Himalayas*?" Elliot asked as he alternated between deep, panicked breaths and feeding bits of pretzel to Jersey. "Not only is it *way* farther than we've ever gone before, but isn't it a remote region with huge mountains and no cities? Do either of you speak Pashto?"

"I will learn to speak it! Right now! Whatever it takes to rescue a unicorn!" Professor Fauna exclaimed.

"What's Pashto?" asked Uchenna.

"It's the language many people speak in

Northern Pakistan. Though Pakistan has a lot of languages. Urdu, Punjabi . . ."

"How do you know all this?" Uchenna asked. "Sorry, silly questio—"

"Last summer I took the encyclopedia out of the public library, one volume at a time. I only made it through *P* before school started, which was a real disappointment. But I read about Pakistan. English is actually an official language of Pakistan, too!"

"Isn't Mount Everest in the Himalayas?" Uchenna asked. "Are we going somewhere near there?"

"On the other side of the range." Professor Fauna let go of the plane's controls, opened up a compartment, and started to fumble with a jumbo map of Asia. Uchenna frantically grabbed the plane's yoke to prevent them from plummeting to the earth.

"The Himalayas span six countries," Elliot

said as the professor wrestled with the map. Reciting facts was helping him feel a little calmer. "Mount Everest is on the border of Tibet and Nepal. Not near Pakistan. But the mountains there are still *huge*."

Professor Fauna said, "We are heading to the Hindu Kush range in the northern region of Pakistan. I think it is there." He pointed with a thick finger at the map. "Specifically . . . *there*. To Torghar. Or the Black Mountain."

"That kinda sounds like the realm of an

evil wizard or something," Uchenna said as she steered the plane over Professor Fauna's outstretched arms and enormous map.

Jersey had finished Elliot's pretzels and fallen asleep on the floor.

"Is there a reason you chose *that* ominously named destination?" asked Elliot. "As opposed to, I don't know, Sunshine Peak or the Be Happy You Definitely Won't Die Here Range?"

"I do not see those on the map," Professor Fauna replied. "Also, after reading Pai Lu's article in the *End Times*, I spoke to Alejandra Cervantes, our friend from Laredo.** She says she has heard of a man they call the Watcher, near Torghar. If anyone would know of unicorns in the Pakistani Himalayas, it would be him! She is sure of it! At last, my life's quest shall be concluded!" Professor Fauna tried to fold the map back up. "*¡Palabrota!* These things are impossible to fold!" He gave up and rolled it into a ball.

** See *The Chupacabras of the Río Grande.*

"Wait, so we're going to a place called the Black Mountain to find a man called the Watcher?" Uchenna asked, giving the controls of the plane back to the professor.

"*¡Correcto!*"

"Why does this seem even more reckless than our typical missions?" Elliot wondered aloud.

"Because this isn't a typical mission," Uchenna replied. "It's way more awesome. We're going to find *unicorns*."

"*¡Encontraremos unicornios!*" Professor Fauna crowed.

CHAPTER FIVE

"Uh, those are *big mountains*." Uchenna was staring out the window, her nose smooshed up against the dirty glass.

"To see bigger ones," said Elliot, "you'd have to go to Mars. The Himalayas are the biggest mountains on Earth." His face was smooshed against the *Phoenix*'s window, too.

Jersey had woken up and was now sitting on Elliot's head. His face was *also* smooshed against the window.

Jagged, snow-covered peaks stretched as far as they could see. The mountains were dazzling against a clear, cobalt sky. Lakes of glacier water glistened; they were a shade of blue none of them had ever seen before.

It was breathtaking, like something out of a dream. Or a documentary. Or . . . a nightmare. Because right at that moment Professor Fauna said, "Time for landing!"

"What? Where?!" Elliot cried. All he could see below him were peaks and patches of snow. There were, in the valleys, tiny collections of cubes that must have been houses, plus a few more scattered up the mountainsides. And the roadways below them looked like tiny threads of tattered twine.

"Yeah, I don't know, Professor," said Uchenna. "I don't see a safe spot for the *Phoenix*—"

"When have we ever waited for a safe spot before?" the professor scoffed. "Besides! There are unicorns down there, waiting to be rescued!

Right now! Can you believe it?! I can't believe it! I am so excited! I have never been so excited in my life!"

"Right. But it would probably *not* be ideal to mow down the unicorns with an airplane," Elliot said, as he and Uchenna scrambled back to their seats and pulled their seat belts tight. Uchenna gripped Jersey to her chest. The plane was angling straight toward a mountainside. It seemed to be *accelerating.*

"Of course! I would never do such a thing!" Professor Fauna shouted, as they plummeted toward the ground. "I would never run over a unicorn!" Then he added: "That child down there, on the other hand, should probably WATCH OUT!"

SMASH! CRASH! WHRRRRRRRRCRACK!

The plane had stopped. Uchenna opened her eyes. She looked down. She was still cradling Jersey in her arms. Elliot was sitting beside her, totally dazed. Professor Fauna was staring out the front windshield.

"Uh, I think we have arrived," he said.

"How's that kid you were about to hit?" Uchenna asked.

"I . . . I have a not-very-good feeling about that. Shall we check?"

Uchenna yanked her seat belt off, threw open the door, and leaped out of the plane. Jersey flapped up above her head, his blue body almost the same color as the sky. His wings looked like two autumn-red leaves borne aloft by the wind.

Uchenna looked under the belly of the plane. All she saw were rough brown rocks.

The plane was, somehow, miraculously, un-scathed, but for a long scratch where it must have run over a boulder that was about a hundred yards behind them.

Maybe the kid was back there?

Uchenna made her way across the rocky mountain, a steep drop to her right, a forbidding slope to her left. She saw no evidence of a child—

Wait.

Uchenna had almost stepped on a flat, beige hat. It looked kind of like a beret woven from un-dyed sheep's wool. She picked it up and turned it around in her hands. Then she scanned the area around them.

She gasped.

There was a body lying facedown a few yards away. It appeared to be a young person.

And it wasn't moving.

CHAPTER SIX

U chenna slowly crept closer to the body, afraid of what she might see. This was bad.

The body wasn't moving.

Very, very bad.

It looked dea—

"BAAHH!" The body sat up and yelled.

"AHHHH!" shouted Uchenna as she jumped back.

"OWWW!" screamed Professor Fauna from the doorway of the plane. He had bumped his head.

Uchenna's eyes were huge as a boy about her age—not small at all, but tall and lanky, with short black hair—stood up and dusted himself off. He wore a long, loose shirt and matching pants that were the same color as the mountain beneath his brown sandals. And he was laughing.

"You almost scared me to death!" Uchenna said, harshly at first, until she remembered that he probably did not speak English. Also that they had almost pulverized him with a plane. Very slowly and loudly, Uchenna said, "ARE . . . YOU . . . OKAY?"

The boy stared at her. She tried again.

"DID . . . OUR . . . AIRPLANE . . . HIT . . . YOU?" She made a little airplane with one hand and tried to illustrate what she was saying.

The boy squinted. Uchenna sighed.

Then the boy spoke.

"NO . . . YOUR . . . PLANE . . . MISSED . . . ME." Then he added, "WHY . . . ARE . . . WE . . . TALKING . . . LIKE . . . THIS?"

Uchenna flushed, incredibly embarrassed. "I'm so sorry. I didn't think you'd speak English. . . ."

"So you thought talking really loudly and slowly would help?" The boy grinned. His English was perfect, with a slight and elegant accent. His eyes were a dark gray, like the rocks all around them.

"I thought we'd hit you. I don't know what I would have done if anything had . . ." Uchenna's voice trailed off as she held out the hat in her hands. "Here."

The boy took his hat and said, "Thank you. I am all right, *Alhamdulillah*. I am Waleed. Who are you?"

"Uchenna," she replied.

Professor Fauna and Elliot had hurried across the steep slope and were now arriving behind Uchenna.

"*¡Lo siento!*" Professor Fauna was shouting. "I am sorry I almost hit you with my plane!"

"We didn't kill him?" Elliot called. "Goodness

gracious, thank heaven! I could have sworn that crunching sound was all his bones breaking!"

Waleed grimaced. "No, my bones aren't broken. But"—he straightened up to his full, lean height—"can I ask you two questions?"

Uchenna, still mortified for assuming he didn't speak English—and for almost killing him—said, "Of course!"

"One: What are you doing here in Torghar? And two"—he leaned closer to Uchenna—"who taught this man to fly a plane?"

Uchenna was about to reply when Waleed suddenly shouted, "Get down!"

Everyone threw their bodies onto the ground. Waleed jumped on top of Elliot.

"*Ow,*" Elliot moaned.

"*What is it?*" Uchenna whispered to Waleed. "*What's wrong?*"

Waleed, pancaking Elliot against the ground, looked truly spooked. "There is . . . a *creature* . . . above our heads. It is like nothing I have ever seen. Perhaps it is a jinn . . ."

They all looked up. Jersey was flapping around in a circle, looking down at them, very confused.

"Ohhh . . . ," said Uchenna. "That's not a jinn. That's our pal. Jersey."

"He's a Jersey Devil," Elliot added.

"A *what*? The *devil*? *Audhubillah!*" Waleed exclaimed, now even more afraid than he had been.

"Don't be scared!" Elliot said. "It's a *Jersey* Devil. From New Jersey."

"We should not be scared of this devil because

it is from New Jersey?" Waleed asked, now completely confused.

"No, there are scary things from New Jersey," Uchenna replied. "The Schmoke brothers, spring break down the shore, the Garden State Parkway at rush hour . . ."

"But not Jersey. He's our buddy," Elliot explained. "Can you get off me now?"

So they all got up, and Jersey came and settled on Uchenna's shoulder, and Waleed could not stop staring.

Professor Fauna cleared his throat. "Waleed, my sincere apologies for almost killing you. I am Professor Mito Fauna. Founder of a secret society whose mission it is to rescue rare and mythical creatures from danger!"

"Creatures," added Elliot, "like Jersey."

"And unicorns!" Professor Fauna added, thrusting his finger into the air.

Waleed said, "Um, if this society is secret, why are you telling me about it? We just met."

"That's a good point," Uchenna agreed.

"Because I trust you!" Professor Fauna exclaimed. "Also, we need your help!"

"Well," said Waleed, "maybe I don't trust *you*. There have been a lot of poachers coming around here recently."

"Poachers?" said Elliot.

"Hunters without permits. Fancy rich guys from other countries, killing our animals."

"We know what poachers are," Elliot said. "They're why we're here. To stop them."

"This," Professor Fauna went on, "is my lifelong quest. To rescue mythical creatures. Specifically unicorns. And they are here. And in danger. We need to rescue them. There is someone here who will help me, I believe. Someone called the Watcher. But I need your assistance in finding him. Will you help us? Pretty please with a cherry on top?" He turned to Elliot and Uchenna. "I just learned that phrase recently. Did I use it correctly?"

Elliot said, "If you were four years old, that

would have been perfect." The professor seemed satisfied.

Waleed's dark gray eyes roved from Elliot to Uchenna to Professor Fauna. "I don't know . . . ," he murmured. Then his gaze settled on Jersey, sitting on Uchenna's shoulder.

Jersey said, *"Eep."*

Waleed bit his lip, then laughed. "Come," said Waleed. "Let us go to my uncle's house."

CHAPTER SEVEN

Waleed led them across the mountainside, moving easily over the rocky path—perhaps aided by his sandals, which appeared to be made completely of rubber. Uchenna thought they were totally punk.

Above them, past the tops of the peaks, the wispy white clouds looked like scarves in the bright blue sky. A large bird of prey circled overhead.

"Golden eagle," Waleed pointed out. "I would

keep your friend Jersey close to you. I don't know if eagles eat Jersey Devils, but they might be tempted to try. . . ."

Uchenna took Jersey off her shoulder and cradled him in her arms. He craned his neck to look around—it seemed like he wanted to glide on the warm updrafts that rose up the mountainside—but Uchenna held him tightly. Professor Fauna was singing a song with absolutely no melody:

"I am going to see a unicorn!
I hope it will have only one horn!
Otherwise it won't really be a unicorn!
Will it? I think not!
Umm . . . spot!"

"There!" he said. "Uchenna! I wrote a song! Just like you!"

Uchenna turned to Elliot. "Do my songs sound like that?"

"Definitely not."

"Good. Because if they did, I would quit music right now."

Uchenna hurried to catch up with Waleed. "Can I say—I didn't expect to find someone who spoke such perfect English way up here in the remote mountains of Pakistan."

Waleed said, "My grandmother has a saying: 'In life, do not expect anything except surprise.' I mean, I *expected* that whoever ran me down in their plane would be some rich and evil poacher. Not a couple of nice kids, their strange teacher, and a blue creature that is not in any of my schoolbooks!"

Uchenna repeated, "'In life, do not expect anything except surprise.' I like that."

"I've been studying English in school since I was little. I also speak Pashto, Urdu, and a little Arabic and Punjabi. And I don't actually live up here all the time. Most of the time I live in Lahore—which is a city of eleven million people."

"Oh! That's bigger than New York City! So . . . why are you here?"

"My grandmother lives here in Torghar with my uncle and auntie, and we visit them every month."

Elliot had caught up with the two kids. "Is Lahore nearby?" he asked.

"It's about a nine-hour drive." Waleed shrugged.

"Nine hours each way? Isn't that really long to do *every* month?"

"Not at all." Waleed looked confused. "My grandmother is so happy to see us. She's getting older and needs lots of medicines. We bring her things that are hard to find here and spend time with her, and with my auntie and uncle and cousins." He waved his arms at the incredible peaks all around them. "And I love it here. It's pretty, and quiet, and the air is so clean compared to the city." He took a deep breath. "Plus, all the wildlife! Eagles, vultures, quail, goats, mountain cats, pit vipers . . ."

"Pit vipers?" Eliott gasped.

"Yes, Himalayan pit vipers. But don't worry—they won't hurt you." Waleed shrugged. "Unless you step on them or something."

"Um, I'm pretty sure pit vipers are super venomous," Elliot said.

"Totally super venomous. One bite and you're dead. So definitely don't step on one."

Elliot gulped and trained his eyes on the ground, making sure that what looked like fallen branches weren't totally-super-venomous snakes.

"Here we are!" Waleed pointed to one of the cubes that Elliot had seen from the air. From up close, it looked more like a rectangular concrete home built into the side of a hill. It was simple, with a door, a couple small windows, and a flat roof. "Welcome to my family's home!"

Uchenna and Professor Fauna came up behind them. As Waleed hurried ahead, Elliot murmured, "It doesn't look like much. . . ."

Uchenna merely replied, "In life, do not expect anything except surprise."

CHAPTER EIGHT

"Please, have a seat." Waleed was pointing to a little dirt-and-grass yard on the side of the house. "This is where we eat when it's warm outside." There were small square stools with embroidered cushions set around a low table.

"Over there is where I play football and cricket with my friends." He motioned toward a larger expanse of grass that was slightly tilted because it was on the side of a mountain. "I'll be right back." He disappeared inside the house.

Professor Fauna settled onto one of the little stools. His knees stuck up at awkward angles, but he sat there, patiently waiting. Jersey crawled under the table, looking for crumbs. Uchenna spotted something leaning against the wall of the house and went to pick it up.

"It's a cricket bat," she said, holding up a wooden-handled paddle. "My cousins in Nigeria play, too. The British introduced it when they colonized Africa. They must have done the same thing here, I guess."

"Cricket?" Elliot asked. "How do you play?"

"It's kind of like baseball. Except the ball bounces on the ground when you pitch it. And there are two wickets instead four bases. And a game can go on for three days. And . . ."

"So maybe not too much like baseball?" Elliot interrupted.

"Well, there's a bat and a ball." Uchenna laughed. "Although you hold the bat upside down."

The grassy cricket-and-football yard connected a few homes. A couple of skinny chickens ran around nearby, and a gray sheep nibbled on a patch of green under a short, gnarled tree. It looked a lot different from their neighborhood in New Jersey, but it was definitely a neighborhood.

They could hear hushed voices from inside the house. After a moment, a small boy in a sweatshirt peeked through the doorway and stared at them with startlingly intense blue eyes. A few minutes later, Waleed came back carrying a steaming plate of rice, a bowl filled with stew, and a pile of circular flatbreads.

"*Noshi jaan sha.* My aunt says she hopes you enjoy this simple food."

Waleed pointed through the door. A short woman with dimples on her cheeks and a red shawl draped over her hair and shoulders was standing in a small kitchen. She smiled and waved shyly. *"Her English isn't very good,"* Waleed whispered. *"But she's very glad you're here."*

"Me too!" Professor Fauna exclaimed. "This food smells like heaven. And we sit as close to heaven as I have ever been," he added, gesturing at the mountain peaks all around him. He took the small plate that Waleed handed him and used a large spoon to ladle the rice and stew onto it. He grabbed a piece of bread. "Ow!" he cried. "Still hot! How wonderful! Ow! Marvelous! Ow! I love fresh bread! Ow! Is this naan? Ow! Ow! Yummy! Ow!"

Uchenna left the cricket bat and joined the rest of the group at the table. Her eyes grew wider after she took her first bite. "This is delicious! I've had naan at restaurants near home, but it's never tasted like this."

Waleed said, "My aunt says when bread is made to feed *Ibn Al-Sabil*, a traveler, it tastes even better."

Elliot said, "*Ibn Al-Sabil*. Is that Pashto? Or Urdu? Or . . . ?"

Waleed, after swallowing, said, "Actually, it's Arabic. From the Quran. We're Muslim. For Muslims, it is very important to welcome and care for strangers and travelers. Please," he said to Elliot, gesturing at the food, "eat."

Elliot took a tiny helping. It smelled too good to worry about the fact that they were eating at a total stranger's house in a foreign country and had no idea what this meal was. The rice was buttery, the stew was nutty and sweet, and the round, warm flatbread was soothing. He ate everything on his plate—but the moment he was done, Waleed was already giving him more.

Waleed gave a piece of naan to Jersey. And then another. And then another. Eventually, Jersey took Waleed's hat in his teeth and pulled it over his blue body like a tiny brown blanket. In moments, he was fast asleep.

"Now that is a use for my *topi* that I have never seen." Waleed laughed.

Waleed kept offering everyone more food . . . though he took only a small portion himself. Even when they were done, he kept insisting they have more and tried to put more on their plates. When they all firmly refused to take another bite, he brought out plump apricots and cups of sweet milky tea that he called *chai*.

"Thank you, and your auntie, for the wonderful meal." Professor Fauna drained his cup, patted his belly with a satisfied expression, and closed his eyes. A moment later, he was sitting upright on the tiny stool, fast asleep.

"Allahu akbar! Allahu akbar!" A voice rang out loud and clear. It echoed in the valley.

Professor Fauna was jolted awake. "Who? What? Where? Why? When?" he cried.

"Ash hadu an la ilaha illah Allah," the melodic voice continued to chant. Jersey's ears perked up even though his eyes were still closed.

Waleed laughed.

"That's the *adhan*, the call to prayer. If you'll excuse me, I'll be back in a few minutes."

Elliot watched as people from the different homes came out and gathered in the open area that Waleed had said was his cricket field

and spread brightly colored woven mats on the ground. They lined up in two neat rows and prayed together, bending, kneeling, and touching their heads to the ground in unison.

"My uncle is Muslim, and he prays like that five times a day," Uchenna whispered. *"He says it makes him feel calm, like meditating does."*

Elliot tried meditating once, in a yoga class his mom took him to. He had tried so hard to empty his head of thoughts that he got a stress headache.

About ten minutes later, Waleed came back toward them with a smile. "After prayers, I spoke to my uncle. He told me where the watchers are today. Not *the* Watcher, though. My uncle has not heard of anyone called that. But the wildlife watchers—them I can take you to."

"That is very kind of you," Professor Fauna said, stroking his beard. "Perhaps the watchers will know who *the* Watcher is. . . ."

"Or maybe we'll wander the Himalayas, not knowing who to talk to, forever," Elliot added.

"If we keep eating meals like that," Uchenna said, "I wouldn't mind."

"So?" said Waleed. "To the watchers?"

"To the Watcher!" Professor Fauna exclaimed. "Or, er, the watch*ers*!"

CHAPTER NINE

The group headed out, and pretty soon, Elliot was panting heavily. Maybe he had eaten too much. Maybe his body wasn't used to the high altitude. Or maybe it was from the excitement of actually getting closer to finding an actual unicorn. It was his turn to carry Jersey, and he coaxed the little blue creature back into his special backpack, safe from vipers and the golden eagles that flew overhead.

Uchenna was composing a song, determined

to show that her songs did *not* sound like Professor Fauna's. Hers was in a key, and was in the style of an uplifting power ballad.

"Among the peaks
Where the sun is warm,
We're on the trail of a unicorn.
The Schmokes killed one,
They stole its horn,
But we'll save the rest
Of the unicorns!"

Waleed's head bobbed to the music.

Professor Fauna exclaimed, "Just like my song!"

It took all of Uchenna's strength not to scream.

Then, Professor Fauna *did* scream. "This is *IT*!"

"What's it?" Elliot asked, grabbing his heart.

"We are *mere moments* away from fulfilling my lifelong quest! Can you believe that this is it?!" Professor Fauna threw his long arms into the air and did a happy dance. He looked like the wacky inflated jumbo balloon man that wiggled outside of Jack's Used Cars back home.

Waleed turned around. "I am sorry to say this, but I don't believe you're going to find any unicorns up here."

"That's what *you* think," Professor Fauna murmured. Then he began laughing giddily to himself.

"Just up this way." Waleed pointed to a small cinder-block building that was very similar to his uncle's house.

"You might want to keep your little devil in that bag, so no one sees him," Waleed added. "You'll get a lot of questions."

Elliot checked on Jersey, who was curled up asleep in the backpack. Then Elliot looked up . . . and froze.

Sitting in front of the little building was a group of men, drinking tea and talking to one another. They were all dressed alike, in belted olive-green jackets and black berets with seals on them. A few were holding notepads. Others had binoculars hanging around their necks. They looked very official. And very serious.

"Those are animal watchers?" Elliot murmured to Uchenna. "They look like an army division."

Uchenna nodded and murmured back, "I know. Something tells me they are *not* going to help us find unicorns."

"Please wait here for a moment," Waleed said. He approached the men and said something in Pashto. Elliot strained to listen. He had no idea what Waleed was saying, but the watchers didn't look like they liked it.

"Maybe we should just go," Elliot whispered to Uchenna. She subtly shook her head.

At least Professor Fauna wasn't dancing around anymore.

As Waleed spoke, one by one the watchers

stopped what they were doing and turned to stare at the visitors. Elliot shifted from one foot to the other. Uchenna gave them a little wave. No one waved back. Or said a word. One of the watchers twirled the end of a very long black mustache and glared in their direction.

Finally, a watcher stood up and sauntered over to them.

"Good afternoon," he said. His English was good, but his accent was much thicker than Waleed's. And his face was as stony as a Himalayan cliff. "What can I do for you?"

"We are looking for the Watcher," Professor Fauna said in his most official-sounding voice.

"Yes. I am a watcher. How can I help you?"

"I mean, *THE* Watcher," Professor Fauna said dramatically. "Where is he?"

"He's the watcher." The man pointed to a man with a mustache holding a teacup in one hand and some kind of cookie in the other.

Professor Fauna gasped, and the man spilled his chai on his lap.

"And also, him." The man pointed to a different man with an even bigger mustache.

"And him, and him, and him," the man continued, pointing at the rest of the group. "We are all watchers. Watchers from the wildlife division of the government."

"But I seek THE WATCHER!" Professor Fauna shouted. It kinda looked like he was about to cry.

The watcher turned to Waleed and said some words the others didn't understand. Waleed replied, shrugging helplessly.

The watcher said to Professor Fauna, his tone gentle, "Would you like to sit and talk? And, please, have some nice hot tea? Are you hungry?" He paused and yelled behind him. "Quick, bring our guests some chai."

Suddenly, the professor collapsed onto the ground. It looked like all the air had been sucked out of his body at once, like the deflated jumbo balloon man outside of Jack's Used Cars.

Everyone gasped. Three watchers jumped to their feet. Uchenna and Elliot were at the professor's side first.

"Is it the altitude?" Waleed asked. "It can have serious effects on those who are not acclimated to it."

Uchenna was leaning over the professor. "Professor Fauna!" Uchenna shook him gently. "Professor!"

Professor Fauna's eyes were wide open, but they didn't blink.

Elliot was about to touch the professor's neck to take his pulse when a low croak emanated from deep in Professor Fauna's throat. . . . "There is no Watcher. Which means there are no unicorns. Which means my life has been a complete and total waste. . . ."

Elliot took the professor's hand. "That's not true, Professor. Don't give up yet!" He turned and looked desperately at Waleed.

Waleed spoke to the watchers for a while. Everyone seemed to have an opinion, including the man carrying a tray with four cups of tea and some biscuits on a plate. Meanwhile, Uchenna and Elliot watched the professor as he murmured about unicorns and his life's mission and whether he'd remembered to turn in his grades for his third-period social studies class and how his whole existence was meaningless.

After a moment, Waleed knelt at the professor's side.

"There might be hope, sir."

It was if Professor Fauna couldn't even hear him.

"Sir, there's another old man who is also a watcher. But he never comes to meetings and doesn't spend time with this group."

Professor Fauna blinked.

"He's by himself a lot. And doesn't speak much. And they think he might be forgetting things in his old age. But maybe it's—"

Professor Fauna sat up like he'd been struck by lightning.

"THE WATCHER!" the professor roared. "In the documents from the Archivo, in Havana, Juanito relayed that unicorns were guarded by silence! Yes! That *must* be him! Let us go! *¡Vámonos, muchachos!*"

Professor Fauna was back on his feet, his eyes wild and his hair coated in dirt and leaves.

"Which way?" he asked Waleed.

"Up there." Waleed pointed to a ragged, forbidding peak, close to the top of the mountain.

Elliot scanned the peak for signs of life. He spotted a tiny hut. "All the way up there? Is it safe? Wouldn't we need oxygen tanks or something?"

The watchers from the wildlife division all started talking at once.

"I wouldn't go up there if I were you."

"You are very likely to fall."

"You should probably have oxygen tanks, yes."

"Take your tea first, please."

"The old watcher up there is slightly demented and maybe a little dangerous."

"See?" Professor Fauna exclaimed. "There is no problem! *¡Vamos, mi gente!*"

And before they could stop him, Professor Fauna was hiking up the steep, scree-covered slope, in his ancient tweed suit and his leather shoes, which looked like they were fancy about forty years ago.

"You said this is a *teacher* of yours?" Waleed asked them.

"Yup," Uchenna replied.

"Your teachers in New Jersey are very different from those in Pakistan."

"Really?" said Elliot. "That sounds nice."

But they hustled up the mountain after their manic, frantic, ecstatic teacher.

CHAPTER TEN

They should have had oxygen tanks.

They started out breathing heavily, but soon, their heads were hurting and everything seemed to be spinning. Every step made them dizzy.

"This is not safe," Elliot moaned, gripping his head as he stumbled along. "We should go back."

"For once," Uchenna said, "I agree with Elliot."

"Are you joking, *amiguitos*?" Professor Fauna said, heaving in and out with every step. "We are rescuing *unicorns*! There is no price I would not pay!"

"How about the lives of your students?" Elliot replied.

"*¡Exactamente!*"

Elliot said, "Waleed, I would like to meet some of these Pakistani teachers you mentioned. Maybe I can transfer into one of *their* secret societies."

Waleed was doing slightly better than the rest of them. "We are almost there. Just keep your eyes on the path. A slip now would be most unfortunate."

Uchenna glanced down the slope of loose

rocks that ran along the path. It dropped steeply for about four thousand feet. She resolved to do as Waleed instructed.

Somehow, miraculously—and after several stops where Elliot declared he refused to go a single step farther—they made it to the hut.

Everyone was exhausted when they got there. Their heads were pounding. They were sweating, but cold, like they had a bad fever or something.

And yet . . .

"This is the most beautiful place I've ever seen," Uchenna said. "No competition."

Elliot breathed deeply. The air was so remarkably fresh and clean, he actually noticed it. He sucked it in like he was drinking nectar.

"There," Waleed said, pointing to the hut ahead. It was maybe half the size of his uncle's home. A man in a watcher uniform and a beret was sitting in a chair in front of the door, fast asleep. His chin was resting on his chest, and his white beard reached halfway down his belly.

"That must be him," he added. "The Watcher."

Professor Fauna straightened his tweed jacket, brushed off his old leather shoes, combed his beard with his fingers, and said, "This is it."

Professor Fauna strode toward the sleeping man and spoke in a booming voice:

"*Perdóneme*, good sir! Are you the man known simply as 'The Watcher'?"

Slowly, the man opened one eye. The eye roved over the professor for a few seconds. Then he closed it again.

This didn't stop Professor Fauna. "*¡Señor!* We need your help!"

This time the Watcher didn't even open an eye. He just kept on sleeping. A snore escaped his lips.

"*It doesn't look like he's watching much of any-thing,*" Uchenna whispered.

Professor Fauna threw his hands in the air and looked like he was about to shake the man when Waleed stepped forward.

Quietly, he moved closer to the man and whispered something in his ear. The Watcher finally opened his eyes.

"Oh, thank goodness!" Professor Fauna exclaimed. "You're awake! Now, we've heard the most alarming story about hunting expeditions! And we have seen the severed unicorn horn. We are here to put a stop to this terrible poaching and to make sure the unicorns stay safe. So." The professor put his hands on his hips. "Can you lead us to where they are?"

The Watcher stared at Professor Fauna and did not reply.

"I, ahem, should mention that we are part of the Unicorn Rescue Society? You might have heard of us? As you can see, I have this identification card. . . ."

Professor Fauna pulled his card out of his wallet and waved it at the Watcher, who stared at him blankly and still didn't say anything.

Finally, Professor Fauna turned to Waleed.

"Why won't he answer? Can he hear me?"

Elliot guessed what was going on. "I don't think he speaks English, Professor."

"It's okay," Waleed added quickly. "I can translate for you."

"Okay." Professor Fauna stood on one side of the man while Waleed stood on the other. "Ask him if he is part of the secret order established to protect unicorns."

"I actually don't know how to say *unicorn* in Pashto," Waleed fumbled. "I can ask if he 'protects the spiral-horned creature of dreams'?"

"*¡Perfecto!*" said the professor. "Close enough!"

As Waleed spoke, the Watcher looked more and more awake, and started to shake his head from side to side.

"No?" Elliot wailed. "No? He doesn't? You mean all of this—flying to Pakistan, climbing a ridiculously tall mountain, and then climbing even higher than that, all of this was for *nothing*?"

"Calm down," Waleed said. "He's saying *yes*."

"Yes? Shaking his head that way means *yes*?" Professor Fauna moved closer to the Watcher. "Ask him if he can take us to them!"

The Watcher shook his head again.

"Hallelujah!" Professor Fauna cheered. He turned and threw his arms in the air. "Finally!"

Elliot nearly collapsed with relief. Uchenna jumped and clapped and cheered.

"He means no," Waleed said in a quiet voice.

"But he just shook his head!" Uchenna said. "I thought that meant yes?"

"Well, it does. But it depends on what the question was."

Professor Fauna made a choking sound and looked like he was about to explode. But, somehow, he kept himself together. "Can you *please* tell him that we are friends? We need to see these animals and make sure they are safe! They could be in grave danger! And we want to help!"

Waleed spoke to the Watcher at length.

The Watcher nodded one way, another way, and a third way as he listened. And no one had any idea what any of it meant.

But then the Watcher slowly stood up out of his chair.

No one breathed.

The Watcher stroked his long, white beard.

They stared.

The Watcher motioned for them to follow him.

Without saying a word, they did.

Elliot glanced at Uchenna and could read her mind.

The moment had finally arrived.

The Unicorn Rescue Society was about to earn its name.

CHAPTER ELEVEN

There were flames running up and down Elliot's legs.

Not literally, but it *felt* like flames were running up and down his legs. On the *insides* of his legs. Also his chest. His chest was on fire. He had never been able to feel the contours of his lungs before, but now he could—he could feel his lungs from the inside out. Elliot swore to himself that he would take up jogging or aerobics or unicycling or *some* kind of cardio workout when he got home so he would never feel this way again—if he just survived climbing this mountain.

The air was so thin and cold and clean, it felt like his throat and lungs were getting cleansed with a freezing cloth with every breath. What was strange about all these feelings is that Elliot never expected to be in such excruciating pain while being somewhere so *beautiful*.

The mountain peaks circled them like turrets of enormous castles.

"This truly is a blessed land," Waleed marveled.

"I'm light-headed," Uchenna said.

"I'm about to die," Elliot added.

"I can ask the Watcher if he'll slow down," Waleed told them. "I don't know if he'll listen." The Watcher was far out ahead, stepping from stone to stone like a mountain goat, holding a simple wooden stick in one hand, completely at ease, despite the fact that he looked older than the professor. He held a loop of black beads on a string in his other hand, clicking them between his fingers as he walked.

Professor Fauna gasped, "No!" More gasping for air. "Do not slow down! We are nearly there! At the achievement of my life's goal! My forever dream! What did you call them? The horned creature of spiral dreams?"

Waleed said, "The spiral-horned creature of dreams."

"Can we let Jersey out now?" Uchenna asked Waleed. "He would LOVE it up here."

Waleed glanced at their guide, far ahead. "I don't think that's wise. Let's wait until we've found the unicorns. I wouldn't want to do anything to upset the Watcher."

"Would it upset him if I *died*?" Elliot asked as he pulled his leg up to the next rock with his arms. "Because I'm pretty sure I'm about to."

Waleed studied Elliot for a moment. At last he said, "No. I don't think it would bother him."

Uchenna laughed. Elliot cried.

Waleed grinned. "I'm just joking. I don't think you'll die, *Insha'Allah*. But try not to. Because yes, it would bother us all very much."

At last, they came to a steep rise, one they could not see over. The Watcher had crouched down near the top of it, and was peering over a large boulder. As Waleed and the Unicorn Rescue Society arrived behind him, he motioned for them to get down with one hand while putting a finger to his lips with the other.

Uchenna glanced at Elliot. Elliot glanced back at Uchenna.

This was the moment.

Professor Fauna's body started jerking like a car trying to drive with the parking brake on. He seemed unable to decide whether to throw himself on the ground to maintain their cover, or to leap on top of the boulder and shout, "Unicorns! At last!"

So he did neither. He just stood there, half bent over, lurching like a broken robot.

"*I think he's losing it,*" Uchenna whispered, gesturing at the professor.

"*Did he* have *it?*" Elliot replied. "*When?*"

They crept up to the boulder where the Watcher was hiding. The Watcher nodded.

"*What does* that *mean?*" Elliot whispered.

"*It means, look over there,*" Waleed answered.

So Elliot, Uchenna, and Professor Fauna slowly raised themselves above the rocks.

"I think I am peeing in my pants," said the professor.

"Me too," Uchenna answered.

They looked down from atop the boulders.

And there they were.

At last.

Spiraling horns.

Many beautiful, long, straight, spiraling horns.

It was a whole *herd* of . . .

"Wait a minute," said Uchenna. "What *are* those?"

CHAPTER TWELVE

"That is . . . *not* what I expected a unicorn to look like," Uchenna said.

"That's because those are *not* unicorns," Elliot replied. "Like, by definition. *Uni-corn* means *one horn*. These things each have *two* horns."

"They look like . . . ," Uchenna murmured, "like . . . *goats.*"

They did look like huge, wooly mountain goats. They had long, brown hair; cloven hooves; the quintessential long pupils that goats have;

and two enormous, straight spiral horns sticking up from their heads. There were six of the creatures. Two were lounging on the ground. Another was standing on top of a rock, looking out into the distance. And a mother was lying on her side, nursing two infants, whose horns had not grown in yet.

"They're amazing . . . ," Uchenna said. "But they're not . . ."

"Unicorns," Elliot completed the thought.

Professor Fauna started to chuckle. They both looked at him. He chuckled some more. And a little harder. "They are not unicorns," he said, laughing a little more loudly now. *"No son unicornios."*

The Watcher came up and tapped him firmly on the shoulder and put a finger to his lips.

But Professor Fauna did not seem in control of his own laughter. He was belly laughing now, and tears were streaming down his face, and now it seemed like he was crying, or maybe laughing, or maybe both. "They're not unicorns!" He laugh-sobbed. *"¡No son unicornios!"*

"Uh, Professor?" Uchenna asked.

"I thought the Schmokes had found them first! And killed one! But they have not! The unicorns are safe! They are safe! And I have NO IDEA WHERE THEY ARE!"

And now he sat down on a rock behind the great boulder and laughed and wept so hard that the Watcher nodded his head at Fauna, and

Waleed translated, in a whisper, *"He wants to know if the professor is all right."* Uchenna and Elliot just had to shrug.

"They're not unicorns!" Professor Fauna was babbling. "The unicorns are safe! And lost! And safe! And I am lost! *¡Soy perdito!* Hahaha-hoohooboohoohahhh!"

"So," Elliot asked Waleed, "what *are* those?"

"Those are—"

VROOOM

Suddenly, all the humans were knocked to the ground.

CHK-CHK-CHK-CHK-CHK-CHK

A helicopter was rising up the mountainside behind them. It rose until it was facing them, its black-tinted windshield staring them down, the wind blowing their hair everywhere and Waleed's hat off his head. The sound was deafening.

Then the chopper turned sideways. It was painted bright, sparkling gold. And across the side were emblazoned the words RECHE FOR YOUR DREAMS!

"*HEY.*" Uchenna tried to make herself heard over the pulsing din. "THAT'S THE SCHMOKE—"

Just then, a window opened up on the side of the helicopter, and a strange-looking weapon emerged.

"IS THAT A CROSSBOW?!" Elliot shouted over the chopper's thunderous noise.

"IT LOOKS A LOT LIKE A CROSSBOW!" Uchenna shouted back.

"ARE THE SCHMOKES ABOUT TO KILL US?" Elliot shouted. "HONESTLY, IT'S ABOUT TIME. I'VE BEEN WONDERING WHY THEY HAVEN'T AL—"

Just then, the crossbow fired right at them.

But it didn't fire an arrow. It fired something

else. Something weird and wobbly. The Watcher, despite his advanced age, suddenly leaped into the air, then he cried in pain and went crashing to the rocky earth, out of sight.

The weird crossbow reloaded and fired again as Waleed screamed and shook his fist at the helicopter.

It hit something on the other side of the boulder, which groaned and then, it sounded like, fell.

The helicopter flew forward, over them, to the far side of the boulder. Waleed jumped up and ran after the chopper, and Uchenna and Elliot and Fauna were instantly on their feet, chasing him. They found the Watcher, lying on the ground, in pain. But he was gesturing at the creatures and shouting, *"Haghuey madad ooka . . . za! Za!"*

Waleed, followed by the members of the Unicorn Rescue Society, sprinted across the stone clearing toward where a creature was lying on its side. They had nearly reached the spiral-horned creature of dreams when it suddenly *rose into the air.*

"AH!" Elliot screamed.

It kept rising, and then they saw that it had a thin rope attached to its legs, and its legs were bound together, and it was fighting and struggling, but the chopper was carrying it away, far away, over the mountain and ultimately out of sight. The other animals had all dashed off.

Waleed and the members of the URS stared after the helicopter for just a moment, and then they hurried back to the Watcher.

They knelt around him in a circle. Waleed was speaking to him quickly in Pashto. Professor Fauna was looking all over the Watcher's torso for where he'd been shot. Elliot was monitoring him for signs of cardiac arrest.

"Guys," said Uchenna. No one was listening to her. "GUYS!"

They all turned to Uchenna. "Look."

She was pointing at a thin black rope that was twisted around the Watcher's ankles, anchored by black weights.

"They shot him with a bola," she said. "Whatever those creatures are . . . the Schmoke brothers wanted one *alive*."

CHAPTER THIRTEEN

Professor Fauna pulled out a pocketknife and swiftly cut the rope off the Watcher's ankles. In just a few minutes, the professor had gone from completely hysterical to calm and in charge.

All it took was the Schmoke brothers' helicopter almost killing them.

Waleed, who looked a bit shaken, used a clean handkerchief to gently dab the dirt off of the Watcher's face. The older man smiled, whispered a few words in Pashto to Waleed, and then turned to Professor Fauna.

"Thank you, friend," he said, in English.

Professor Fauna smiled. "You are welcome, *mi amigo*." He reached out his big hand, and the Watcher clasped it, and the professor pulled the Watcher up into a sitting position. They sat beside each other, two men with big beards. Both were tall and angular. Both serious. They looked like they could have been brothers.

At just that moment, a ferocious sound erupted . . . from inside Jersey's backpack.

"He's still in there!" Uchenna exclaimed.

"He's probably freaking out," said Elliot. They looked to Waleed. "What do you think? Would it be okay if . . . ?"

Waleed shrugged. "It's up to you."

Meanwhile, the Watcher seemed to be following their conversation. Or at least he realized that there was a debate going on about the contents of the backpack.

He leaned forward curiously.

Uchenna unzipped the backpack.

Jersey burst out, flapping and hopping up and down and growling in all directions.

"Shh! Jersey! It's okay! Everything's all right!" the kids tried to assure him.

The Watcher leaped backward and threw his arms around Professor Fauna. Professor Fauna hugged the Watcher back. Not because he was scared, but because he liked hugs.

"*Hagha sa shay dey?*" the Watcher demanded.

"He wants to know what it is," said Waleed.

"*Kho da khalaq di sok?*" the Watcher went on.

"He wants to know who you *really* are," Waleed added. "Also, you called the helicopter 'smoke brothers.' Why? What is actually going on here?"

"*Schmoke brothers.* And I had a question for *you*," said Elliot. "Those creatures were *not* unicorns. So what were they?"

Waleed smiled. "It seems that we both have information that the other wants." He turned to the Watcher and spoke in Pashto for a moment. The Watcher nodded diagonally and replied. Then he pulled a silver thermos from his satchel. "He says that we will provide the refreshment, and you will explain yourselves first."

The Watcher took a few small metal cups from the top of his thermos. And then, to everyone in the Unicorn Rescue Society's surprise, he poured steaming cups of hot tea and passed them around.

"Tea? He has hot tea at the top of a mountain?" Uchenna asked. "Nice touch."

"Do not expect anything except surprise." Waleed smiled. "Like I said, taking care of our guests is important to us. So is drinking tea. And since I was almost killed by something flying at me for the second time today, a cup of tea sounds good."

Elliot could have used more than tea. He wanted a hot water bottle, his bed, and to dig his old, worn stuffed rabbit out from his closet and cuddle it. His stomach felt like it was wrapped in a bola, and he thought he might throw up. But since tea was his only option, he clutched his cup with both hands and sipped it slowly as Professor Fauna explained to the Watcher, with Waleed translating, about the Unicorn Rescue Society.

And, miraculously, the tea helped.

CHAPTER FOURTEEN

Uchenna expected the Watcher to be skeptical when Professor Fauna told him about their secret society—since there appeared to be no mythical creatures around here—just those goat things with the incredible, unicorn-like horns. But the Watcher didn't seem doubtful at all. Maybe because Jersey was perched on a boulder above their heads, the fur on his face blown back by the mountain breeze, his back and neck stretched. He looked like he was posing for a postcard.

As Professor Fauna spoke, the Watcher listened more and more intensely, clicking the string of black beads in his right hand.

When he finished explaining the Unicorn Rescue Society, Professor Fauna leaned back. "Now it's your turn, Mr. Watcher. I want to know everything about those amazing double-horned creatures!"

"*And* what those beads do," Elliot quickly added.

Waleed smiled. "The beads are for *tasbih*. They don't do anything. We just use them to remember God throughout the day, between prayers."

Without warning, the Watcher reached out and handed the beads to Elliot. Elliot hesitated at

first, but then took them and examined them. A simple string held the glassy beads together, and a long tassel hung off the end. He clinked them a few times like the Watcher did, bunched them together in his palm, and handed them back.

"They're cool," Elliot said.

But instead of taking them back, the Watcher shook his head and smiled.

"They are yours now," Waleed explained.

"Oh no," Elliot stammered. "I can't take them. They're his. And besides . . . I'm Jewish."

The Watcher chuckled and answered softly when Waleed translated.

"It's a gift," Waleed explained. "He wants you to have them. And, he says, Jews and Muslims are brothers in faith." Waleed leaned closer to Elliot. *"Also, I would not refuse a gift,"* he added in a whisper. *"That's not done here. He will feel insulted."*

Elliot nodded. "Thank you," he said as he slipped the beads into his pocket. Elliot made a mental note to remember to take them out before putting his pants in the laundry. Explaining a million prayer beads in the washing machine to his mom would not be easy, especially considering she thought he was in Miss Vole's classroom right now.

"Also," said Waleed, "the Watcher says you can call him by his name, Asim. I call him Asim Sahib. It's like Mr. Asim."

"Asim Sahib," said Uchenna and Elliot at the same time.

Professor Fauna chimed in. "Mr. Asim Sahib. I got it."

Waleed shook his head. But the Watcher, Asim Sahib, smiled.

"To answer your other question, these double-horned animals are called markhors," Waleed translated as Asim Sahib started to speak again. "They are the national animal of Pakistan and a symbol of strength."

"They are . . . uh . . . *goats*, right?" Uchenna asked. "Because they sure looked like gigantic goats."

"Yes. Markhors are a special type of mountain goat. They only live in the Himalayan mountains, and different kinds of markhor have distinctly shaped horns. These are Suleiman markhors, known for their beautiful spiral cone horns."

Asim Sahib began speaking again in a soft voice, taking several long pauses to let Waleed translate.

"These mountains used to be filled with thousands of mighty markhors. But years of war in Afghanistan next door led to lots of people and lots of guns coming into these parts of Pakistan. Many markhors were hunted for food, fur, and horns, until eventually there were only a couple hundred left."

"They're nearly *extinct?*" Elliot gasped, his heart sinking at the idea. Jersey turned his head, as if he understood the question, and fluttered down into Elliot's lap. Elliot stroked the blue fur of his head.

"Well, they were endangered," Waleed said,

and then continued translating Asim Sahib's words. "Something had to be done. This area is governed by tribal leaders, who agreed to ban hunting of the markhor. With the help of the United States Fish and Wildlife Service, actually, they set up the Wildlife Watchers program. The Quran says that the human is the guardian of God's creation. That is why Asim Sahib became a watcher, he says. He wants to honor our tradition of treating animals with kindness, not wasting water, and planting trees that bear fruits."

"So," said Uchenna, "the program made a difference?"

"The conservation efforts are working, and now there are a few thousand markhors again. They aren't even on the endangered species list anymore."

Uchenna frowned, deep in thought. "So, if the animals are protected, what are the Schmoke brothers doing here?"

"There are still some very rich people who come here to hunt," Waleed said sadly. "A few are allowed to buy permits from the government each year. And then there are poachers who do it illegally. They are the worst. That's what I thought you were when I first saw your plane."

"Us? Gross. Never!" Uchenna wrinkled her nose.

Suddenly, Elliot realized something. "I don't think whoever was in the Schmoke helicopter was hunting, either! They wanted to capture the markhor alive, right? But why?"

He waited for Waleed to ask Asim Sahib. Waleed listened to the Watcher's response and shook his head like he couldn't agree with what he was hearing. Waleed started to object. Asim Sahib shook his head and said something that sounded like *yes*. Or it could have been *no*. They continued arguing. And after what seemed like forever, because Elliot had finished his tea by the time they were done, Waleed turned to them.

He said: "You're *not* going to believe this."

CHAPTER FIFTEEN

Waleed crossed his legs and began settling in like it was story time.

Elliot and Uchenna, who both firmly believed that you're never too old for story time, got comfortable, too.

"*Markhor* means 'serpent eater' in Persian," he said. "These mountain goats got that name because they are known to kill pit vipers."

Elliot stopped getting comfortable. "Okay,

now I love them." Then his eyes scanned the ground around them, just in case.

"Yeah, markhors stomp on pit vipers with their big hooves and kill them dead." Waleed smashed one hand into the other like he was crushing something in it.

"Serpent eaters? So then they *eat* the dead snakes?" Uchenna asked, with a look of utter disgust.

"No. Goats eat plants. They're vegetarians."

"Oh, right. Okay." Uchenna shook her head slowly. "But then why'd they get that name?"

"It's just a name."

"Well, it's a pretty bad name," Uchenna said. "And by bad, I mean *baaad*, as in *awesome*. Serpent Eaters . . . That's not only a good *goat* name . . . it's also a good *band* name!"

Suddenly, she grabbed an invisible microphone.

"Hello, MetroPark! We are the Serpent Eaters! RRROAAAHHHHHH!"

Uchenna started playing imaginary drums and head-banging, her twists flying everywhere.

Asim Sahib had never seen anything like it. He was very confused.

But Waleed wasn't. He joined in: "And the first album is called 'Serpent Eaters Sanctuary'! Which is what this wildlife protection area is literally called! This is a song from our new album, 'Serpent Eaters Sanctuary'! RRRROAHHH!" He joined Uchenna with the head-banging and

shredded an air guitar. Jersey started prancing all around them like a tiny hard-rock band mascot. If hard-rock bands had mascots.

Elliot decided that the altitude, and almost getting killed by a rogue golden helicopter, was getting to them.

Professor Fauna pressed Waleed for more information. "What else can you tell us about these markhors?"

"Oh, so many things!" Waleed continued to play his air guitar as he rattled off facts about the markhor and Jersey continued to dance. "The male markhor can grow to be over two hundred pounds! Their fur changes color in different seasons! They have amazing balance and can get up the steepest rocks without falling! I've even seen some climb trees—"

"Goats climbing trees? I'm sure that is an incredible sight," Professor Fauna cut Waleed off. "But I'm afraid none of this explains why the Schmoke brothers are after them."

"Well, there *is* something else that's pretty unbelievable," Waleed said. He stopped playing his air guitar and grew serious. Uchenna reluctantly gave up her head-banging and picked up her steel teacup. "After markhors eat, sometimes there's a frothy foam that develops around their mouths, and then falls to the ground. When it dries out, it hardens into something that sort of looks like a rock."

"Not to be rude," said Elliot, "but that's . . . *not* unbelievable. It's just kinda gross."

"Yeah, well, here's the unbelievable part. And it's *also* kinda gross: some local people used to believe that the dried foam has the power to cure snakebites and some types of illnesses," Waleed went on. "They would hold it over a snakebite, to supposedly draw the venom out. Or they'd soak it in their tea and drink it."

Uchenna had just been about to take a sip from her teacup. She froze. Jersey had been dancing, but he froze, too.

"Don't worry." Waleed laughed. "There's no goat cud foam in there."

But the professor was getting excited. "But did it work? Can this cud neutralize the venom from snakebites?"

Waleed turned to Asim Sahib, who spoke some more.

"He doesn't think so," Waleed reported. "Asim Sahib says mixing cud with tea is a very old-fashioned belief, and if you're not careful, you could get really sick from ingesting strange parts of animals. Also, he said, sometimes a stone of the hardened cud foam is found in the markhors' stomachs, after they die."

"Stop," said Elliot.

Waleed looked at Elliot nervously. "What's wrong?"

"Did you just say that you can find the cud stone *in a markhor's stomach*?"

"Yes . . . that's gross, too, I suppose. But not grosser than drinking—"

"So it's a BEZOAR!" Elliot shouted.

Everyone was knocked backward by Elliot's sudden enthusiasm.

Uchenna said, "What are you shouting about, Elliot?"

"A *bezoar*! It's a bezoar!"

The whole group stared at Elliot, mystified.

"You don't know what a bezoar is?"

Everyone shook their heads.

Elliot took a deep breath. "Ooookay. Listen. Bezoars are awesome. They were used in Europe hundreds of years ago in alchemy, which everyone thought was *magic* but just turned out to be the predecessor of chemistry. They were brought from Persia, now known as Iran—which is right next door to Pakistan! Goodness gracious! This is amazing. I read in a very old book that the name *bezoar* comes from the Persian words *pa*, against, and *zahar*, poison! I don't speak Persian, so I don't know, but it *sounds* plausible. Also—"

"Does he always talk like this?" Waleed asked.

"If you get him going," Uchenna said.

Asim Sahib was getting excited, too. He spoke, and Waleed translated: "The stone made of markhor cud is called Zaharmora!"

"IT'S THE SAME THING!" Elliot screamed.

"Why are you so excited about this?" Uchenna wanted to know.

"It's just that bezoars are really important in alchemy, magic, and the history of medicine. And they actually work! Sort of. They don't actually work against snake venom, but if you put a bezoar in a liquid with arsenic in it—arsenic is a really bad poison, in case you didn't know—the bezoar will actually draw the arsenic out of the liquid through a process of chemical bonding!" Elliot looked around at the group, his eyes wide, his chest heaving.

"Uh . . . I think you should calm down. You look like you're about to hyperventilate," Uchenna told him.

"Okayyyyyyy . . . ," said Waleed, slowly. "So . . . a Zaharmora is a kind of bezoar. Cool . . . Aaaaany- way . . . ," he went on, waiting to see if Elliot would leap in with more random facts about be- zoars. When Elliot restrained himself, Waleed told them, "Asim Sahib says there's a rumor that someone was recently making the rounds of the villages, asking all sorts of questions about Za- harmora, and willing to pay a high price if they could produce one that really worked."

"AHA!" Professor Fauna shouted so loud that Waleed jumped.

"That's it," Uchenna said. "That's got to be it."

"Wait," said Waleed. "What has to be what?" The Watcher was nodding in all sorts of direc- tions at once. Maybe he was trying to follow the rapid-fire conversation. Either that or he was at- tempting to head-bang.

Uchenna turned to Waleed. "The Schmokes are after—"

"A BEZOAR!" Elliot shrieked.

VROOOM!

Everyone instantly flung themselves to the ground. Jersey flung himself on top of Elliot's face. "Ow," moaned Elliot.

CHK-CHK-CHK-CHK-CHK-CHK

The RECHE helicopter flew over them—still suspending the poor, frantic markhor beneath it. It swooped down the mountainside and accelerated.

"Quick!" Professor Fauna shouted. But he didn't have to. Because Jersey was already flying after the helicopter, his tiny red wings flapping frantically through the thin mountain air.

"Wait, Jersey!" Elliot cried.

"Go Jersey!" Uchenna shouted.

"What should we do?" Waleed asked.

But Asim Sahib was already springing over

rocks and sliding down scree slopes like he was a mountain goat himself.

Uchenna and Elliot looked at each other.

"We should go after them! Fast!" said Uchenna.

"But be careful of pit vipers!" added Elliot.

"Okay," they said at once. "GO!"

Waleed and the members of the Unicorn Rescue Society sprinted after the Watcher, trying to keep up with the old man.

CHAPTER SIXTEEN

The golden chopper was soon far out ahead of them. It could fly directly over the deep valleys between mountain peaks, whereas the Unicorn Rescue Society had to circumnavigate them on foot. Jersey remained a beacon for them, though, a blue-and-red dot that never let the helicopter out of his sight, but also stayed within view of Elliot and Uchenna.

After some time, the RECHE helicopter disappeared around a nearby peak.

"We've lost them!" Waleed cried.

"I don't think so," said Uchenna. "It looked like the chopper was landing over there."

"I hope so," gasped Elliot, "because I *cannot* go much farther."

Soon, they had caught up to Asim Sahib. He put his finger to his lips again, and then gestured for them to follow. There was a narrow dirt path that traveled around the mountain peak.

It was so narrow, in fact, that they all had to walk heel to toe. Which seemed to be no problem for the ancient Watcher. But it was very difficult for Elliot, Uchenna, and Professor Fauna. Especially with the gusts of wind that would suddenly push them from behind.

Elliot peered down the steep mountain slope. A tiny river ran through the valley far below. "If we fell down there, we would definitely die," he said.

"Oh yes," Waleed agreed. "Definitely."

Just then, the wind shoved Elliot forward.

Uchenna grabbed him just before he went toppling head over heels down the mountain. "So," Uchenna said, "don't."

"Right. Good advice."

Asim Sahib led them onto a flat plateau, protected on two sides by a rounded cliff face. The plateau was filled with large, khaki-colored tents, the kind with four sides, peaked roofs, and flaps for doors. In the middle of the all the tents, the helicopter stood, cooling down, its rotors slowing but not quite stopped. The markhor, and whoever had been in the helicopter, were nowhere to be seen.

Asim Sahib did not have to put his finger to his lips this time. They knew. They all crouched down and began to sneak through the camp. On the roof of each tent were the words SCHMOKE BROTHERS RARE AND EXOTIC CREATURE HUNT-ING EXPEDITIONS. The tents had windows—made of thick, clear plastic. The group made sure to stay low enough to the ground that anyone inside wouldn't see them.

They crept up to the nearest tent. Professor Fauna peered inside.

It was empty.

They crept to each tent and peered inside.

But all the tents were empty.

Where had the people in the helicopter gone? And where was the markhor?

Finally, they came to two central tents that were larger than all the others. Uchenna peeked in the window of one of them.

"*Whoa*," she whispered. "*It's like a fancy bedroom in there. Two fluffy-looking beds, two plush* sitting chairs, two changing areas behind two folding screens . . ."

"Two of everything, huh?" Elliot murmured. "I can't believe it."

"Yeah," agreed Waleed. "How weird is that?"

"It isn't weird at all," said Elliot.

"It's not?"

"No," he said. "It's the Schmoke brothers."

"Quickly!" Professor Fauna hissed. "Come here!" He was peering in the window of the other large tent.

The Watcher, Waleed, and the members of the Unicorn Rescue Society quickly and silently gathered around and peered in the foggy tent window. Jersey fluttered above their heads, trying to see, too.

There, gathered around the window of a large tent way up in the Himalayas, they watched the Schmoke brothers do the most cruel, dark-hearted, evil thing they had ever seen them do.

Which was really, *really* saying something.

CHAPTER SEVENTEEN

The captive markhor was bound and tied in a corner. There was a local man, wearing a hat very much like Waleed's, crouched over the animal.

In another corner, there stood a boy, not much older than Waleed, who was holding a black box.

The Schmoke brothers' butler, Phipps, was sitting in a chair. One leg of his black satin trousers was rolled up. And he was sweating.

Milton and Edmund Schmoke were standing above him.

"Now, Phipps, remember, you must report to us *exactly* how you feel," Edmund was saying. Edmund was short and round and looked very much like a toad.

"Yes, sir."

"We must know the effects of the antidote *exactly*," added Milton, the tall, angular brother. "There's no one else we trust to give us a perfectly accurate description."

"Thank you, sir. I am honored, of course, sir."

Phipps did not *look* honored. He looked terrified. He mopped his brow with a handkerchief. His black butler's bow tie was soaked through with sweat.

"Ali, come!" Edmund barked.

The boy stepped forward. The Schmoke brothers stepped back. Phipps continued to sweat.

"The legends of the Himalayas tell us that this will work!" Milton reassured Phipps.

"It better," Edmund muttered to his brother. "For *his* sake." And he jerked his head at their butler.

"Of course, sirs," Phipps replied, his teeth now chattering. "I am certain that your sources are perfectly reliable."

"I'm glad *he's* sure," Milton said out of the side of his mouth. Edmund nodded.

Peering through the window, Asim Sahib muttered something. Waleed translated: "He doesn't know what they're about to do, but he's pretty sure it's a terrible idea."

Inside the tent, Ali, the boy, said, "Are you ready?"

"We're ready!" chorused the Schmokes.

Ali squinted sympathetically. "But are *you* ready, sir?" he said to Phipps. "You're certain? This seems like a very bad idea to me."

"Who asked you?!" Edmund Schmoke bellowed. "You're the help! So is he! No one asks the help's opinion!"

Ali looked at Phipps. Phipps pursed his lips and nodded bravely.

Ali exhaled. He put the black box on the floor. The Schmoke brothers took another step back. Ali gripped a handle on the box.

"Do it already!" Edmund barked.

"I can't watch!" Milton cried.

Ali pulled up on the handle. One side of the black box opened.

Slowly, a head emerged.

The head of a pit viper.

Outside the tent, Elliot murmured, *"Goodness gracious . . ."*

And Waleed began to pray.

CHAPTER EIGHTEEN

The pit viper tested the air with its tongue. Behind its yellow eyes were the two enormous divots in its face that gave the pit viper its name.

"Quickly!" Edmund Schmoke bellowed. "Kick it! Before it gets out of the box!"

Phipps inhaled sharply through his nostrils. Then he kicked the pit viper in the face.

The snake lashed out, sank its fangs into Phipps's calf, and then recoiled into the box for safety. Ali slammed the lid of the box shut.

"Well?" Milton said. "How do you feel?"

Phipps was, very clearly, in shock. He was barely moving. His eyes were wide. And the area around the viper bite was swelling quickly.

"Not . . . ," said Phipps, ". . . very well . . . sirs. . . ."

"Good!" Edmund turned to the man in the corner of the tent. "Now quickly, Zarar! The cud foam!"

Outside, Asim was speaking very urgently and very angrily. Waleed did his best to relay the gist of what he was saying. "This is the stupidest thing he's ever seen. It's an ancient legend, but everyone knows now that a Zaharmora won't cure a snakebite. In fact, it's likely to give that poor man some other virus. If he doesn't die from the snakebite. Which he almost certainly will."

Zarar hurried to Phipps, while Ali retreated with the black box. Zarar dipped the white, frothy foam of the markhor into a cup of tea, and brought the tea to Phipps's lips.

"It's not even a bezoar! It's just the foam!" Elliot exclaimed.

The sweating butler sucked the tea down, while his eyes rolled back in his head.

"*Ya Allah, ya Allah*," Ali and Zarar were both praying loudly.

Outside the tent, so were Waleed and Asim Sahib. Uchenna and Elliot were saying, *"Please don't die please don't die please don't die . . . ,"* under their breath. Professor Fauna was just staring, stunned. And Jersey had hidden his face. He couldn't watch.

Edmund and Milton Schmoke came closer. Zarar backed away. Phipps swallowed the whole cup down. His head began to loll this way and that. His enitre leg was turning red.

"His calf is puffing up like a pillow!" Uchenna hissed.

"That means there's a lot of venom in there," Elliot replied. *"He's likely to have trouble breathing*

now. He may even be having a heart attack. We need a defibrillator!"

"We don't have one of those," Waleed whispered.

Milton was now leaning over Phipps. "So? Is it working?"

No answer.

"Report, Phipps, blast it all, report!" Edmund snapped.

Phipps managed to make some gargling sounds.

"It isn't working!" Milton moaned.

"Argh!" cried Edmund. "What a waste!" He turned on Milton. "What a complete waste of time and resources! I always knew RECHE wasn't worth the effort!"

"It would have been . . . had the markhor antidote worked!" Milton retorted, straightening up and facing his brother. "We could have countered the cockatrice poison in our lab in Switzerland! *And* made a profit on the hunting expeditions!"

Edmund waved his hand dismissively.

"Hunting is *stupid*. Why *kill* an animal when you can *profit* from it? I mean, sure, if you can profit off helping *other* people kill it, that's *okay*. But the margins just aren't worth the effort!"

He stormed out of the tent, and Milton hurried after him. "But listen here, you're judging the experiment now that you know the results! If it *had* worked—"

The members of the Unicorn Rescue Society watched in disbelief as the Schmoke brothers argued all the way to their own tent and disappeared inside.

All while their most loyal servant, their butler, their right-hand man, Phipps, was *dying*.

"*What are we going to do?*" Elliot whispered.

"What do you *mean*, what are we going to do?" Uchenna replied. "We're the Unicorn Rescue Society, aren't we? Let's *rescue* somebody!"

CHAPTER NINETEEN

U chenna sprinted around the corner of the tent and burst inside.

The man, Zarar, and the boy, Ali, were both trying to revive Phipps, who had passed out. Zarar was still praying. Ali was crying.

The Watcher came into the tent right after Uchenna and started ordering Zarar and Ali around in Pashto. He pointed at the markhor, and Ali hurried to release it from the bola wrapped around its legs. Elliot started doing chest compressions on Phipps, to make sure his heart kept beating. Professor Fauna put his mouth to Phipps's leg to try to suck the venom out.

"Wow," Elliot said, in the middle of chest compressions, "*that* is commitment."

"I thought he was your enemy," Waleed said.

Professor Fauna spit on the ground and said, "This is the difference between the Schmokes and us, Waleed. They harm, we rescue. Whatever—*and whoever*—needs rescuing."

Uchenna had lifted Phipps's head and was staring into his eyes. "He's in really bad shape. This markhor cud is *not* magical at all."

Asim Sahib straightened up. He started speaking rapidly to Zarar. Zarar nodded vigorously.

Asim Sahib turned to Waleed and spoke to him. Waleed, in turn, spoke to the members of the Unicorn Rescue Society.

"Can you carry him?" Waleed asked.

"Of course!" Professor Fauna replied.

"Good! Then bring him to the helicopter."

"Are we taking him to a hospital?" Elliot asked.

Waleed turned and asked Asim Sahib, who replied rapidly.

"No," said Waleed. "We're taking him somewhere closer."

"Where?"

"We're taking him to the markhors that *are* magical."

CHAPTER TWENTY

Elliot's heart was pulsing in his throat as he ran behind Uchenna to the helicopter. Professor Fauna and Zarar were half carrying and half dragging the unconscious Phipps in front of them. Waleed and Asim Sahib were in the rear. Jersey flew around them all, a blue-and-red blur.

In the commotion, Elliot didn't have the chance to get nervous about riding in a helicopter. Or maybe he was too busy being terrified by the possibility of watching someone *die* in front of him. He quickly strapped on his belt while the chopper blades were spinning. Zarar lifted them off the ground.

"WHAT DO YOU MEAN 'MAGICAL'?" Elliot shouted to Waleed over the roar of the helicopter engine and rotors. It sure sounded like that was what Waleed had said just moments ago. But now that he thought about it, it didn't make any sense.

"WHAT?" Waleed shouted back.

"MAGICAL MARKHORS?" Elliot screamed louder. "Where are they? What do they do? Can they help us? Is Phipps going to die?"

But Waleed pointed to his ears and shrugged. He couldn't make out anything that Elliot was saying. And Elliot realized that he might barf if he didn't clamp his mouth shut. The helicopter was lurching off the ground.

Elliot was certain that there was no such thing as magic. Creatures had abilities that often seemed magical—but were really the products of millions of years of evolution. Chameleons can change colors depending on their surroundings. Homing pigeons can use the earth's magnetism to find their way home from miles away. If we didn't have the sense of smell ourselves, the ability to detect a fresh pie from a block away would seem magical, too. And mythical creatures—well, their evolutionary abilities tended to be even more astounding.

Elliot looked at Phipps, slumped in a seat, his head lolling to one side. His eyes were rolled back in his head. If it weren't for the slight shaking of his arms, Elliot would have been convinced that he was already dead. Whatever these special markhors' evolutionary abilities were, they were going to have to be as powerful as magic, or the Schmokes' butler was a goner.

Waleed had handed Uchenna a cloth, which she was using to wipe Phipps's head. She had a look of determination Elliot had seen before. He

wouldn't have been surprised if she could somehow keep Phipps alive through the sheer force of
her will.

Professor Fauna was checking Phipps's pulse
and counting so loudly that everyone could hear
him, helicopter noise and all. Whether they could
understand him was another question, because
he was mixing English and Spanish, apparently
too anxious to notice. "*Vente*-two, twenty-*tres*,
vente-four . . ."

Asim Sahib was calm, his palms raised in front of him and lips moving as he recited prayers. Jersey rested on his lap, watching curiously. This did not seem to bother the Watcher.

Zarar was a good pilot, and the helicopter moved swiftly off the mountain peak and toward another. Even as his nerves made his insides twist like a propeller, Elliot couldn't help but notice the spectacular scenery surrounding them. It was surreal, especially compared to the horrific scenes that kept playing on repeat in his mind:

The pit viper. The bite. Phipp's swollen leg. And the almost-dead man drooling right in front of him. The almost-dead man . . . who'd been their enemy since before Elliot had even known there was such a thing as the Unicorn Rescue Society. Who they were trying to save. *In life, do not expect anything except surprise.*

Suddenly, the sound of the helicopter changed from a smooth *CHK-CHK-CHK-CHK-CHK-CHK* to a loud, slapping *THWACK-THWACK-THWACK*. It sounded like something was stuck in the propeller and stopping it from turning. Elliot clenched his eyes shut and howled.

"We're going DOOOOOWN!"

And they were. But not into the fiery heap that Elliot feared. Instead, Zarar was landing the helicopter on a small grassy patch on a different mountain—the highest peak for miles and miles.

And when they stopped moving and Elliot opened his eyes, he didn't even have to ask Waleed again what he'd meant by "magical markhors."

He began reconsidering everything he'd thought about mythical creatures and their evolutionary abilities.

The helicopter was surrounded by goats that looked one hundred percent *magical*.

CHAPTER TWENTY-ONE

About a dozen markhors filled the grassy area. They were either pure white, spotted brown and white, or a golden tan color. They were mostly bigger than the first group of markhors.

And their beautiful spiral horns were *glowing*.

Or maybe it was just that their horns were perfectly smooth and shimmering, like a pearly shell that caught the light and reflected every color of the rainbow. But it sure *looked* like they were glowing.

"Whoa." Uchenna whistled under her breath as she climbed out of the helicopter. "Check that out!"

"*¡Madre mia!*" Professor Fauna exclaimed as he stumbled out of the helicopter under the weight of Phipps, whom he was carrying on his back. He fell to his knees. "Look at these beautiful creatures! They look like unicorns! Two-horned unicorns! They are . . . *duocorns!*"

Phipps made a moaning sound just then. He could have been agreeing with the professor. Or he could have been trying to say, *Hurry up already, I'm dying.*

"Hurry up already, he's dying!" Waleed cried. "What do we do?" Asim Sahib gave instructions to Waleed, who yelled out translations.

"Okay, lean him against this boulder here."

Professor Fauna and Zarar propped Phipps up. His face was a deep shade of purple now, and Elliot was afraid that the butler wasn't breathing.

"Now we need to get one of these markhors to come closer to us," Waleed said, relaying Asim Sahib's instructions.

The nearest markhor was at least twenty feet away. In fact, it was amazing that the helicopter hadn't sent them all running farther away, but they seemed to be intrigued by the commotion and the strange, shouting creatures who had emerged from the giant bird with the rotating wings above its head.

"Come here, duocorn! Come, you great big adorable horned creature of spiral dreams!" Professor Fauna made kissing sounds with his lips and motioned with his hands.

The markhor that Fauna was calling looked like it might have been a juvenile, since its horns weren't as enormous as some of the others. It stood perfectly still and blinked its large eyes.

"Here, markhor, markhor. Here, boy . . . ," Uchenna joined in after she had handed the thermos to Asim. She slapped her legs and pleaded with the markhor to come.

The markhor still didn't move.

"Maybe they like salt, like deer!" Elliot suggested. "Let's give it some salt."

Waleed said, "That's a great idea! There's very little salt in the mountains. All the creatures up here go crazy for it."

"Yes, but where are we going to get a salt lick from?" Professor Fauna asked, looking around as if one might suddenly appear.

But Elliot was already unzipping the backpack. "I have pretzels!" Jersey immediately flew over, expecting a treat. Uchenna had to grab him and hold him back. Elliot pulled out a bag that had once contained pretzels . . . before Jersey had eaten them all.

"Oh no . . . ," Elliot moaned.

"This could still work!" Uchenna grabbed the bag and pulled out a handful of crumbs and salt from the bottom. Then she crept toward the markhor and sprinkled a small trail of salty pretzel fragments as she backed away.

The young markhor blinked at the trail of crumbs.

"You can do it . . . ," Uchenna murmured, Jersey still clutched in her arms.

"Follow the pretzel crumbs . . . ," Elliot said.

"Like Hansel and Gretel . . . ," Waleed added.

"You know Hansel and Gretel?" Elliot asked.

"Everyone knows Hansel and Gretel," said Waleed.

The young magical markhor was still blinking at the pretzel crumbs. He was really cute, with his tan coat and sparkling horns. What made him less cute was that behind them, Phipps was dying in the arms of Zarar and the Watcher. And whatever this markhor was supposed to do to save him, he *was not doing it.*

"Come *on*, little guy . . . ," Uchenna moaned. "Or," she said suddenly, "should I say, *big guy* . . ."

CHAPTER TWENTY-TWO

An enormous male markhor, with the longest horns any of them had ever seen on an animal, had started walking forward. Uchenna and Elliot instinctively took a step back. This guy was *huge*. And he looked *mean*.

He pushed the young goat out of the way, planting his forehead on the kid's butt and shoving him, so the young one went stumbling clumsily off to the side. It was almost funny.

Then the huge markhor walked straight up to the salt trail and . . . started licking it.

He licked it, and licked it, and walked right toward them.

"It's working!" Uchenna cheered.

The salt trail brought the markhor closer and closer, and the humans backed away, making sure to keep a safe distance from the enormous goat.

When the markhor was only a couple of feet away from the tree where Phipps was, Asim Sahib announced something. Waleed translated: "Now for the hard part."

"None of *that* was the hard part?" Elliot exclaimed, incredulous.

Asim Sahib barked at Zarar and Ali, and then at Waleed. Waleed turned to Professor Fauna. "Go help them."

Zarar and Ali grabbed Phipps's legs and they lifted them into the air, upside down. Professor

Fauna, following Asim Sahib's instructions as relayed by Waleed, grabbed the dying butler around the waist and hoisted him as high into the air as he could.

Elliot and Uchenna watched, stunned. "This is the weirdest thing we have ever done," Elliot said.

Phipps looked like a floppy mannequin.

Asim Sahib approached the markhor slowly, speaking softly in Pashto and gently stroking his

fur. His head was bent, vacuuming up salt and pretzel crumbs, but he was so large the top of his shoulders came up to the middle of Asim Sahib's chest . . . and the horns were as high as his black beret.

The Watcher motioned for them to bring Phipps closer. They staggered forward. Asim Sahib gently touched one of the markhor's glowing horns. Fauna, carrying the bulk of Phipps's weight and sweating like a melting snowman, took one step closer. Then Asim Sahib took Phipps's swollen, red, upside-down leg in one of his hands and guided it until the puffy red snakebite was less than an inch from the pearly horn.

At which point, something very miraculous started to happen.

A clear, viscous liquid began to ooze out of the wound, as if attracted to the horn. It dripped down Phipps's exposed leg and fell to the ground at Asim's feet. The markhor, who was licking up salt, saw it and began to lick up the venom, too.

Elliot tried to jump forward to stop the markhor from ingesting the poisonous venom—but Waleed put out an arm and stopped him.

"Animals, I find," said Waleed, "tend to know what they're doing."

Uchenna murmured, so, so softly, *"Hello, MetroPark—we are the Serpent Eaters . . ."*

And Elliot said, *"Ohhh . . ."*

They waited for what felt like forever, watching the markhor's horn draw the venom from Phipps's leg—drip, drip, drip—and the markhor lick it up.

Finally, there seemed to be no more venom left. And all the salt was gone. The markhor's soft lips explored the ground until he found Asim's shoelaces. He started happily munching on those, while the men gently laid Phipps on the mossy rock of the mountaintop.

"Did it work?" Elliot asked.

"I . . . hope so . . . ," Fauna heaved. "Because otherwise . . . my chiropractor . . . will be mad at me . . . for nothing. . . ." He collapsed on the ground beside Phipps.

Who was not moving.

Who looked completely and totally dead.

"It didn't work . . . ," Waleed moaned.

"It has to work!" Elliot burst out, surprising himself. He felt his throat constrict as he watched. He wanted to bury his face and sob.

"Give it time . . . ," Uchenna said, arms wrapped so tightly around Jersey he could barely breathe.

Just then, Phipps started to cough.

They all froze.

"What . . . *cough* . . . in . . . *cough* . . . the world?" Phipps sputtered.

His face was turning less purple. His eyes opened.

"*Cough* . . . why . . . *cough* . . . were you holding me . . . *cough* . . . upside down . . ." He sat up. ". . . and *hugging* me?!"

Everyone cheered, while Phipps stared at them in a daze.

"AH!" His eyes had focused on Professor Fauna. "*YOU* were hugging me? NOOOOOO!"

CHAPTER TWENTY-THREE

Waleed tried to explain to Phipps that Professor Fauna and the rest of them had just saved his life. But the butler did not want to hear it.

"I can't be seen with you!" he kept saying. "The masters would sack me for sure!"

Uchenna freed Jersey, and he went swooping around their heads. She walked up to Phipps. "Now, you listen here, you sniveling zombie servant!" Phipps looked shocked at that description. "The Schmoke brothers let a pit viper bite you, just to test if some goat spit could save you—and it *couldn't*. They didn't have any other antidote up there! They were going to let you *die*!"

Phipps pulled himself up and made his upper lip look very stiff. "Nonsense. The masters just had faith that I would be strong enough and loyal enough to recover!"

"*Recover?!*" Elliot exclaimed. "You were pretty much *dead*!"

"Well, I'm not now!" Phipps said, straightening his black jacket and bow tie, which were now filthy with venom, saliva, and dirt. "I'm alive and . . . *say*, how *am* I alive? Was it that strange upside-down hug, or what?"

Phipps's eyes fell on the giant markhor, who had taken a break from chewing on Asim's bootlaces to watch the whole scene with apparent interest.

"That doesn't *look* like the other markhor we captured . . . ," Phipps said.

"You're hallucinating," Uchenna said quickly.

"Am I?" Phipps replied, his eyes narrowing. "Or . . ."

CLANG.

Phipps crumpled to the ground. The Watcher stood over him with his thermos of tea. It was now dented where it had hit Phipps on the head.

They all sat down in a circle, and Asim passed out the steel cups again, and they shared tea while they discussed what to do with Phipps.

Waleed wanted to keep him for ransom. "Don't let him go until the Schmokes promise to leave here forever!"

"They are leaving anyway," Professor Fauna countered. "They think the experiment was a failure."

"But now Phipps might tell them about these magical markhors," Uchenna replied.

"They're *not* magical," said Elliot. "Though that evolutionary adaption to their horns is *amazing*. It must work like the bezoar, drawing poison through a chemical—"

"ENOUGH WITH THE BEZOARS, EL-LIOT!" Uchenna shouted.

"Sorry."

"Do the other watchers know about these extraordinary creatures, too?" Professor Fauna asked. Waleed translated.

Asim Sahib smiled his mysterious smile again, and said just a few words.

"He's kept them a secret from the watchers and the community for many years," Waleed explained. "For now, no one else knows about them, or their powers."

The huge markhor had decided that Elliot was the saltiest of the group. He kept trying to lick the back of Elliot's neck, or his arms, or any other exposed part of him. Elliot would shriek and leap up as soon as he felt the markhor's hot breath on his skin. Not because he thought the markhor was dangerous—just because it's freaky to have such a huge creature trying to *lick* you. And also, he was worried the markhor would chew on his hair.

So as they had this conversation, Elliot kept leaping up and changing places in the circle. And wherever he went, the markhor would follow.

And Jersey hopped along behind the great goat, following the glow of his spiraling horns.

Phipps lay there, unconscious. His body was likely grateful for a chance to rest and recover after the trauma of the snakebite.

Having finished his third cup of tea for the day, Elliot really had to go to the bathroom. Waleed told him he could pee on any rock—the moss under their feet was fragile and rare, but the rocks made excellent toilets. The urine would evaporate quickly.

Elliot went away from the group, and the markhor followed him.

"Go away!" Elliot said to the markhor. "Can a guy get some privacy? Even up here?" He looked around him. Besides his friends, there were no other humans for miles. Just stunning snowy mountains and deep, jagged valleys.

He went a little farther, and the markhor decided to sit down and wait for him. Relieved, Elliot relieved himself.

Then, as he started back toward the group, the markhor walked straight past him.

"Where are *you* going?"

And then he saw something even more disgusting than all of the disgusting things he'd just witnessed.

Elliot hurried back to the group, gagging.

"What?" Uchenna asked, seeing Elliot's face.

"I think urine has a lot of salt in it, because that markhor is—"

Just then, they heard:

CHK-CHK-CHK-CHK-CHK

Everyone leaped to their feet.

"The Schmoke brothers!" Uchenna cried.

"No! It's Phipps!" Professor Fauna shouted. "He's getting away!"

Phipps had come to, it appeared, and snuck off to the chopper. He had started the engine, and the Unicorn Rescue Society could do nothing but shield their faces from the wind as he lifted the great metal bird off the mountaintop.

"Come back here, you pit viper!" Waleed called, shaking his fist.

Phipps did not come back. But as the helicopter rose into the air, Elliot thought, maybe, that he heard something shouted against the din.

It sounded a little like the words "THANK YOU."

Or maybe it was just the roar of the rotors.

CHAPTER TWENTY-FOUR

"What if he tells the Schmokes about the special markhors?" Elliot asked, squinting at the helicopter as it disappeared over the Himalayan peaks. "Are they just going to start all of this again? Are we going to have to *stay* here?"

Uchenna was glaring after the chopper, her fists on her hips. After a moment, she said, "I don't know. But I kinda think . . . he won't."

"That's optimistic of you," Elliot replied.

All Uchenna could say was, "In life, do not expect anything except surprise."

Waleed was speaking excitedly to Asim in Pashto. The old man took his hand and spoke to him as they started back down the mountain.

Elliot and Uchenna waved good-bye toward the great markhor—but he was too busy licking a rock to notice them. So Professor Fauna went up to the goat and began murmuring in his ear. The markhor ignored him.

As they slowly trekked back to Asim's hut, Uchenna asked the professor what he'd said to the markhor.

Professor Fauna smiled. "I said, *amiguito*, that he may not be a unicorn. But, nonetheless, meeting him was the thrill of a *lifetime*." And he exhaled.

During the hike, everyone was quiet, lost in their thoughts and trying to process what they had just witnessed. Except for Jersey. He was flying over their heads in great loops, finally able to enjoy the mountains' updrafts. He could handle a golden eagle, they figured. They were learning that, together, they could handle just about anything.

When the group reached Asim Sahib's home, he invited them inside, and the group settled onto thick, colorful cushions with little mirrors sewn into them that were arranged around a low table. The furnishings were simple but warm, and included clay pots and a beautiful green-and-gold Quran resting on a stand. The Watcher disappeared into another room and returned with a carved wooden tray that he set on the table. It was filled with metal bowls overflowing with pistachios, dried apricots, and raisins; thick, buttery tea biscuits; and a fresh pot of steaming chai.

"I must tell you all something," Waleed said. "I had an idea at the top of the mountain. I thought: My grandmother is sick. We drive nine hours each way to bring her medicines. And yet,

the greatest medicine I've ever witnessed is right here in Torghar. Why can't we use the markhors, somehow, to help her? And why shouldn't we tell the world about their great magic?"

The Unicorn Rescue Society grew quiet. It was a good point. But something about it made them all feel uneasy. . . .

"I told this to Asim Sahib, and he helped me understand," Waleed went on, as he helped pass around the bowls and pour the tea. "These special markhors must be kept secret. If word got out about their powers, people would come from all over the world to capture and exploit them. And, just like what almost happened with the regular markhors, they could very quickly be wiped out—forever."

Professor Fauna nodded thoughtfully and slurped his tea. "Yes, I'm afraid that's true. Greed is a powerful force."

"Asim Sahib said he has used their powers only once before today—the day he discovered them, in fact. He had found these markhors and then, on his way down the mountain, been bitten by a viper. He remembered the story of Zaharmoras drawing venom from a wound, and these special markhors' amazing horns, and he dragged himself back up the mountain. It was the only way to save his life. But these few animals can't take the place of modern medicine for billions of people. And they can't stop people like my grandmother from aging, which is natural." Waleed sighed. He gestured toward the Quran. "Like our holy book says, 'Indeed we belong to Allah.' There is only so much we should try to control."

"Your grandmother is lucky to have such a loving family to take care of her," Uchenna said gently, as she cracked open a pistachio.

"We are lucky to have someone as wise and thoughtful as her," Waleed replied.

"Speaking of grandmothers," Elliot said. "Mine is going to wonder where we are if we don't get home soon." He drained the last drops of his final cup of chai and fed Jersey the rest of his biscuit. He felt a tug in his heart as he looked over the silver bowls and steaming cups of tea at the Watcher and Waleed.

They hiked down to where they'd left the *Phoenix*. Somehow, it was still totally intact despite their previous flight, which had never happened before, and it was as sky-worthy as it ever was. Which was not very.

As everyone gathered around the plane, Waleed stood near Uchenna and Elliot, hugging himself, clearly trying not to look too sad. Jersey flapped his wings in front of Asim Sahib's face, and the older man bobbed and weaved, shadowboxing with their little blue friend, laughing.

Professor Fauna called everyone over to him. He had fished something out of the back of the *Phoenix*. It was hidden in his closed fist.

Uchenna, Elliot, Waleed, and Asim Sahib

gathered around. Jersey perched on Waleed's head. Waleed laughed and let him stay there.

"I must tell you," Professor Fauna said, "there were times during this journey when I felt that all was lost. When I thought that my adversaries—who are more evil than I had even imagined!—had won the race to find the unicorn, and had done terrible things to the creature of my dreams. But you, Waleed, and you, Asim Sahib, you restored my hope that we will still find the unicorns—*somewhere*. For perhaps these markhors are their distant relatives!" Professor Fauna continued, "And you also reminded me that we who believe in caring for others, for animals, for the planet—we are more powerful than the Schmoke brothers, and more powerful than all those who follow their selfish philosophy. They always expect to win. But they should know to expect nothing from life but surprise."

Waleed grinned.

"And so . . ."

Professor Fauna opened his fist.

". . . I wanted to ask you both . . ."

Sitting on his broad palm were two silver rings. They were each emblazoned with the silhouette of a unicorn. The words *Defende Fabulosa* and *Protege Mythica* circled the icon.

"Would you join us—the newest members of the Unicorn Rescue Society?" He looked at

Waleed. "We need young people who are brave and kind and willing to drag a dying man into a helicopter and help extract venom with the horn of a maybe-magical goat. We need people like that."

Waleed grinned. "When you put it that way, it makes me think that you don't have many other candidates. I guess I have to say yes."

"And you, Asim?" Professor Fauna asked. "You have been working to protect these creatures for a long time, so you are sharing in our work already. Shall we make it official?"

The Watcher shook his head.

"No?"

The Watcher nodded.

"Yes?" Professor Fauna said. "Wait, I am very confused."

The Watcher sideways-nodded. Then diagonally shook his head. Then he gave them a thumbs-up. A thumbs-down. And finally, one of each.

"Uh . . . ," said Professor Fauna.

"What is going on?" Uchenna whispered. *"Is he saying yes or no?"*

Elliot said, *"I have no idea."*

And then Asim Sahib broke out laughing. Waleed guffawed.

"What? What is happening?" Professor Fauna demanded.

Asim Sahib spoke in Pashto. Waleed, wiping away tears of laughter, said, "He was messing with you. He says, 'Yes, I would be honored.'"

So Waleed and Asim Sahib put on their rings, while the rest congratulated them—and asked them to be sure to call them if the Schmokes returned. Then the Watcher presented Professor Fauna with a few more gifts to take home—small sacks of dried fruits and nuts and a package of loose tea leaves—which the professor accepted happily. The two men hugged, and as he stepped back Asim Sahib placed his hand over his heart and bowed his head in farewell.

Finally, the visiting members of the Unicorn

Rescue Society and Jersey loaded themselves onto the *Phoenix*. They all smooshed their faces up against the windows to take a last look at the magnificent landscape. And to wave good-bye, one last time, to their new friends.

A HISTORY OF

The Secret Order of the Unicorn

(Being the History of the Secret Organization, Founded in the Year 789, That Exists to Protect Unicorns from All Humans Who Might Hurt Them)

e've got to rescue the unicorns!" Eva screamed.

The members of the Secret Order of the Unicorn ran up a steep, grassy slope, out of a valley surrounded by towering, snow-covered mountains.

Welf, Eva's brother, was out front. "You're sure it's up here?" he panted. "I don't see any big stone buildings . . ."

"It's hidden from view!" Alcuin replied. He was an older man, in his long black monk's robes, and he was starting to fall behind. Gisela, a young nun, grabbed Alcuin's arm and yanked him forward. Alcuin was still talking as he struggled to keep up. "The monastery is a secret! And the monks who live there are the best secret keepers in the world . . ."

"Then why," asked Khaled, who had his little sister Lubna in his arms, "are we leading an *army* right to them?" Khaled looked over his shoulder, down into the valley. He could not see the horsemen.

But they were there. And that they were getting closer.

"Because," puffed the young nun Gisela, pulling Alcuin to get him running again, "otherwise we'll *die*. And, worse, so will the unicorns." Gisela was cradling her little gray bunny in one arm as she ran.

All around them, a thousand unicorns were streaming up the mountainside, trampling the green grass and millions of wildflowers underhoof.

The unicorns were much faster, of course, than the six humans—Alcuin, Eva, Welf, Gisela, Khaled, and Lubna—and the herd surged past them, up the slope. Within minutes, all of the unicorns were over the top of the hill, and out of sight.

There was still the sound of hooves, though. Behind them. Hooves that did not belong to unicorns.

Their pursuer. And his posse of hunters.

Finally, Alcuin and the crew made it to the top of the hill. In front of them was a small stone monastery, nestled under snowy mountains. Here, monks could live far, far away from the rest of the world, praying and reading and praying some more.

The herd of unicorns mulled around the meadows that surrounded the building, cropping grass and wildflowers. Wildflowers, little Lubna had discovered, are unicorns' favorite food.

Lubna wriggled out of Khaled's grip and ran to play with a young unicorn she'd befriended. Khaled called her to come back, but she wouldn't.

"She's probably safer with the unicorns than with us," said Eva.

Just then, from below, they heard horses coming up the hill.

"Quick!" Welf cried, and they sprinted across the meadow as fast as they could, to the large wooden door of the monastery. Alcuin banged on it with his fist. "Let us in! It's Alcuin! I am a friend of the abbot! Let us in!"

But it was too late.

Thirty spears appeared over the top of the hill. Then the straight ears and long heads of horses. Then the hunters themselves, clad in thick leather and bristling with weapons.

And at the center of them, the largest hunter of all.

Emperor Charlemagne.

Eva and Welf reached out and held hands. They had started this adventure two years ago, when they'd convinced Alcuin to help them save a single unicorn from the most powerful man in the world. That would be Charlemagne. Now, they had saved over a thousand unicorns, and brought them to this place high in the mountains to keep them safe from anyone who would hurt them.

From people like Charlemagne.

They thought Charlemagne had forgotten them.

Clearly, they were wrong.

"My dear friends," the emperor said. He didn't have to yell for his voice to carry across the meadow. He was the tallest man any of them had ever seen, and his chest was as large as an old oak's trunk. Charlemagne means Charles the Powerful, and also Charles the Very, Very Large. Both meanings of the name were accurate.

Emperor Charlemagne led his horsemen forward.

Eva started walking toward them. Khaled, Gisela, and Welf followed Eva.

The unicorns had stopped grazing. They were all staring at the horsemen, their eyes wide, their ears alert. Somewhere among the unicorns, Lubna was hiding.

The Secret Order of the Unicorn met

Charlemagne and his hunters in the middle of the meadow. A group of heavily armed warriors versus four kids.

"You have stolen my unicorns," Charlemagne said in a deep voice that echoed off the mountains all around them. "Did you think I'd not notice?"

"We won't let you hurt them!" Eva shouted. *Hurt them . . . hurt them . . .* echoed through the valley.

Charlemagne threw his head back and laughed. "How will you stop me? No one has ever stopped me. I have conquered the whole world. What are *you* going to do?"

His horsemen chuckled and grinned at their leader.

Charlemagne went on, "Every king in Europe is my servant now. These unicorns will serve me, too."

"Yeah, to stop you from vomiting all over the place," Welf muttered.

A hunter snickered, and then stifled

the sound with his sleeve when he saw Charlemagne's expression.

Just then, tiny Lubna ran out from behind Khaled.

She stood right in front of Charlemagne's towering horse.

She was holding a bouquet of flowers.

The hunters started to laugh. "She looks just like my kid," one of them said.

Khaled started for his little sister—but Eva stuck out a hand and held him back. He had not seen what Eva saw.

Charlemagne peered down—way, way down—at tiny Lubna with her pudgy cheeks and adorable dimples. He smiled. "Do you think, tiny girl, that your bouquet of flowers will prevent me from killing your friends here? Because, as sweet as you are, it won't."

But the flowers were not for Charlemagne. They were for the unicorns.

A black foal Lubna called Bariq pushed past the members of the Secret

Order of the Unicorn and came to stand beside her.

Then the foal's parents came forward. Then more unicorns pushed past the kids, to form a line between Charlemagne and the members of the Secret Order of the Unicorn.

Lubna had led them all, with a single bouquet of wildflowers.

Charlemagne forced a laugh. "It won't take an hour to slaughter every one of these creatures." He wiped his hand on his pant leg, like maybe it was getting sweaty, before taking a firmer grip on his sword.

Charlemagne might have been getting nervous. His hunters were downright scared. "Uh, your majesty . . ." one said. "I'm not so sure."

Dozens and dozens of unicorns had gathered around now, pointing their horns at the men. Hundreds more were watching the scene warily.

"Bye bye bad men!" Lubna called.

"We're not leaving," said Charlemagne.

Which is when the line of unicorns started marching forward. Past little Lubna.

Step. Step. Step.

The horses that Charlemagne and his men were riding had to shuffle backward.

"Yes," Khaled grinned. "You are."

Step. Step. Step. The unicorns advanced.

Charlemagne's horses scuttled back farther. They were becoming scared, and the men were doing all they could to prevent their horses from panicking.

Which is when a noise came from across the meadow. Eva, Gisela, and Welf turned to look. Khaled hurried forward and scooped up little Lubna.

The noise was the sound of the monastery door, opening at last.

They heard Alcuin call across the

meadow: "Anyone who lays down his weapons is welcome!" *Welcome . . . welcome . . . welcome . . .* echoed off the mountain faces and through the valley.

"Men, prepare for battle!" Charlemagne growled.

"With the unicorns?" said the hunter beside him.

"And the children! Cut them all down!"

The knights looked to one another, uncertainly.

Gisela, gripping her bunny to her chest, said, "Has it ever occurred to you that these unicorns are parents, children, sisters, brothers, grandmothers? And you're going to kill them?"

One of the hunters said, "My grandmother is a saint!" He sounded like he was going to cry.

"Humans are animals too," Gisela went on, gripped her bunny tighter.

"Preposterous!" Charlemagne snapped.

But Gisela wasn't talking to him. She was talking to his men. "Hurt animals," said Gisela, "and you're hurting yourself."

Step. Step. Step. The unicorns continued to advance, like a phalanx of soldiers—except their weapons were spiraled and *glowing*. The knights' eyes were roving everywhere, vacillating between indecision and panic.

"Steady, men!" Charlemagne growled.

And then, there was a clang of metal.

One of the leather-clad knights had thrown his spear.

To the ground.

It was the one who had said Lubna looked like his daughter. He quickly dismounted his horse and dropped his shield and the sword that had hung at his side, too.

"This way," said Eva, and she reached out to him from the other side of the line of unicorns.

The hunter quickly hurried toward her—and the unicorns parted to let him through.

The man right beside Charlemagne saw this and quickly threw his weapons to the ground as well, slid from his horse, and hurried after his comrade, through the line of unicorns.

The one with the saintly grandmother also dismounted and discarded his weapons. As he approached Eva, she said to him, "Welcome to the Secret Order of the Unicorn."

The man had a big brown beard and yellow teeth and a huge scar over one eye. He looked down at her—and smiled.

And then every other hunter threw down his weapons, jumped off his horse, and walked through the tunnel of unicorns.

"Come on," said Welf. Khaled and Lubna and Gisela went with the knights across the meadow to the monastery.

Eva stayed behind.

Charlemagne did, too.

He was too shocked to move.

"I— I—" he stammered. "How *could* they? I am Charlemagne! The most powerful man in the world!"

The unicorns stepped forward again.

Charlemagne's horse looked like it was thinking about deserting him, too. It nervously pranced backward, even as he jerked the reins to keep it steady.

"You may be the most powerful man in the world," Eva replied, "but you're still just a man."

Suddenly, the black foal lunged forward. Charlemagne's horse panicked. It turned and took off down the steep hill as Charlemagne shouted for it to stop, and then pleaded for it to stop, and then howled in fury as he realized that he couldn't even control his own horse, much less a thousand unicorns—or a single little girl.

Up at the monastery, the door had opened, and the abbot was waving them all inside. "Thank you," said Khaled.

As everyone else hurried inside, Welf stood watching his sister walk across the meadow, back toward them. The unicorns were grazing and frolicking in the bright green grass, under the snowy mountain peaks and the blue sky.

Eva waved to him, and he waved back. They were both grinning.

Alcuin looked at the wall of towering mountains all around them. He sighed in a satisfied way.

"I bet these unicorns won't be found for a thousand years!" he said.

And he was right.

It took just about one thousand three hundred years for someone outside of the monastery to find them . . .

ACKNOWLEDGMENTS

THIS BOOK WOULD NOT HAVE BEEN POSSIBLE without Hena's baby brother Azim Khan, who alerted her to the existence of the fascinating markhor, along with the folklore that surrounds it. Thank you, Azim, for joining the Unicorn Rescue Society and launching this adventure! Hena's sister Andala Khan and brother Omar Khan joined the fun too and helped out by reading our draft manuscript and fact-checking cultural and religious references. Afgen Sheikh pitched in by adding useful notes.

Hena was lucky to be able to turn to her global network of cousins, which proved to be a wonderful resource throughout the writing process. Seher Naveed Sherazi generously connected us to her cousin Hesham Khan, who answered a million questions on the various horn-shapes of markhor, the region, local customs, and more. Farah Burki came through for us by getting us Pashto translations with the help of her friend Sonober Khan.

As always, Hena is thankful for her husband and sons for their love and support through the brainstorming and writing process, and to her mother, who encouraged her to read, dream, and believe in magic.

HENA IS ALSO INCREDIBLY HONORED that Adam invited her to write this book with him, and grateful for his kindness and friendliness from the first time they met, and for the way he's been a tremendous advocate of her writing ever since. She's so glad that we had the chance to chat about mythology and jinn and our love of writing on a tour bus filled with authors, and that it led to us taking this amazing journey together.

ADAM COUNTS HIS LUCKY STARS that Hena agreed to join the Unicorn Rescue Society. It has led to many, many laughs, as well as a wonderful book, and a lasting friendship.

AND EVERY ONE OF THESE ACKNOWLEDGMENTS should have mentioned Hatem Aly, without whom the URS would not look at *all* like the URS, and would be 98% less awesome. Thank you, as always, Hatem for your art and your genius.

Hena Khan grew up devouring books, but never saw herself represented on the pages. That's why she set out to write characters that share her Pakistani American Muslim identity—in the hopes that other kids will feel seen in her work. Hena's groundbreaking picture books include *Night of the Moon, Golden Domes and Silver Lanterns*, and *Under My Hijab*. Her debut middle grade novel *Amina's Voice* launched Simon & Schuster's Salaam Reads imprint and was named a Best Book of 2017 by the *Washington Post, Kirkus*, NPR, the Chicago Public Library, and others. Her subsequent novels include *More to the Story*, the Zayd Saleem, Chasing the Dream series, and *Amina's Song*. A native of Maryland, Hena lives in Rockville with her family. But she loves to travel to exciting new places and once even flew in a plane about the size of the *Phoenix*.

WHEN ADAM INVITED ME to write this book with him, I was thrilled to go on an adventure to the country of my parents' origin, Pakistan. As someone born and raised in the US, but proud of my heritage, I loved the idea of this series taking us across the globe and offering a lens to explore a culture and place that is a part of me. And if that included a search for unicorns, I was ready to go!

By absorbing only what we are shown in the news, it's pretty easy to get a limited view of northern Pakistan—often one that's filled with conflict and poverty. But in reality, there's so much more to the region. And Pakistanis have many wonderful things to be proud of, like their country's stunning natural beauty, rich history, loving extended families, and delicious food. That food includes the yummy flatbread known as "naan," which we never ever call "naan bread." That's because it's just "naan."

While writing this book, I was also glad to include elements of Islam, a major world religion that stresses the importance of generosity, compassion, and conserving nature. I was hesitant at first, but Adam encouraged me to add more of my faith in each draft. I'm grateful that he did, since the culture of Pakistan is intertwined with it. Adam also suggested introducing the concept of Ibn-al-Sabil, the welcoming and feeding of travelers, a core value for Muslims. We made a joke of the constant serving of chai, which should never ever be referred to as "chai tea." It's just "chai." But seriously, hospitality is a big deal in

Pakistan (and having food piled on your plate means you really should eat it).

It was also fascinating to get to know the markhor, the national animal of Pakistan. Like the Pakistani people, it is powerful and resilient. I hope to visit the mountains of Torghar on my next visit to Pakistan, and to see these beautiful creatures thriving in the wild thanks to multinational conservation efforts. And I hope we can continue to protect these and other threatened species—both real *and* magical. Finally, I hope that we can all make the effort to appreciate our differences, find common ground, and learn from each other—preferably while breaking naan together and enjoying some nice, hot cups of chai!

—H.K.

Adam Gidwitz taught big kids and not-so-big kids in Brooklyn for eight years. Now he spends most of his time chronicling the adventures of the Unicorn Rescue Society. He is also the author of the Newbery Honor–winning *The Inquisitor's Tale,* as well as the bestselling *A Tale Dark and Grimm* and its companions. He is also the creator of the podcast *Grimmest.*

Jesse Casey and **Chris Lenox Smith** are filmmakers. They founded Mixtape Club, an award-winning production company in New York City, where they make videos and animations for all sorts of people.

Adam and Jesse met when they were eleven years old. They have done many things together, like building a car powered only by a mousetrap and inventing two board games. Jesse and Chris met when they were eighteen years old. They have done many things together, too, like making music videos for rock bands and an animation for the largest digital billboard ever. But Adam and Jesse and Chris wanted to do something *together*. First, they made trailers for Adam's books. Then, they made a short film together. And now, they are sharing with the world the courage, curiosity, kindness, and courage of the members of the Unicorn Rescue Society!

Hatem Aly is an Egyptian-born illustrator whose work has been featured in multiple publications worldwide. He currently lives in beautiful New Brunswick, Canada, with his wife, son, and more pets than people. He has illustrated many books for young people, including *The Proudest Blue: A Story of Hijab and Family* by Ibtihaj Muhammad with S. K. Ali, the Newbery Honor winner *The Inquisitor's Tale* by Adam Gidwitz, the Unicorn Rescue Society series also by Adam Gidwitz with several amazing contributing authors, the Story Pirates book series with Geoff Rodkey and Jacqueline West, early readers series Meet Yasmin with Saadia Faruqi, and *How to Feed Your Parents* by Ryan Miller. He has more upcoming books and projects in the works. You can find him online @metahatem.